GW00870058

Also by Susan Gabriel

Fiction

The Secret Sense of Wildflower
(a Kirkus Reviews Best Book of 2012)

Lily's Song
(Sequel to *The Secret Sense of Wildflower*)

Temple Secrets

Trueluck Summer

Seeking Sara Summers

Circle of the Ancestors

Nonfiction

Fearless Writing for Women

Available at all booksellers
in print, ebook and audio formats.

Quentin and the Cave Boy

Susan Gabriel

Wild Lily Arts

Quentin and the Cave Boy

Copyright © 2014 by Susan Gabriel

All rights reserved. No part of this book may be reproduced or transmitted in any form or by any means without written permission of the author, except in the case of brief quotations embodied in critical articles and reviews.

ISBN 978-0-9835882-2-1

Published by Wild Lily Arts

To the Dream Maker

The Dream

"Quentin, are you up yet?"

The Voice yelling up the stairs is my mom's. I've heard it for the last twelve years of my life, and I've got to tell you, I'm getting tired of it. It's there when I wake up. It's there when I go to bed. Sometimes I even hear it in my sleep, like a recording of everything she's ever said to me has soaked into my brain cells or something. To think that same voice used to sing me lullabies! And like most babies who drool in a crib all day, I probably loved it.

I wish Dad still lived here. Dad's voice doesn't bother me at all. He used to wake me up on school days, but not at the crack of dawn like Mom. Six months ago, Dad moved to Oregon—three thousand miles and three time zones away—with the waitress at the diner who used to serve us blueberry pancakes every Saturday morning. That leaves me, my mom, and my sister, Katie, who is four years and three months older than me. As the only guy in our family, I'm outnumbered two to one.

I can tell you're still in bed, Quentin," *The Voice* yells. Not only can her vocal chords penetrate steel, but she has X-ray vision, too. The clatter of bowls and silverware in the kitchen adds exclamation points to her words. My dog, Coltrane—named after my dad's favorite jazz sax player, John Coltrane—

licks my face, like he's trying to warn me. I crawl deeper under the covers and drift off to sleep for one last dream:

A Stone Age kid sleeps on the floor of his cave and pulls a bear hide around his shoulders. His mom grunts from overhead, "Boy, get up." The cave woman is missing teeth and looks like a dirty, primitive version of my mom. The voice sounds familiar, too.

The boy rolls over and looks like a dirty, primitive edition of me. He grunts and goes back to sleep.

The cave mom yells a prehistoric version of "Get up!" She throws a pile of animal bones in his direction. They clatter to the floor inches away from his head.

"Quentin, get up!" *The Voice* yells at exactly the same time.

Startled awake, I sit up straight in bed. In the next instant it's like the dream and real life collide, because somehow— don't ask me how—the cave boy crosses from his world into mine and is now sitting on the end of my bed. Coltrane begins a low growl behind his teeth and starts sniffing like crazy in the direction of my dream.

"Hey, what's happening?" I say. I rub my eyes to wipe away the mirage in front of me. Surprise, it doesn't go away.

Cave boy grunts. He rubs his eyes, too.

"I'm dreaming," I say to myself.

We stare at each other. In a way it's like looking in a mirror, but a really old one, where one of my ancient ancestors is glaring right back at me. And a mirror where I'm having the worst hair day of my life and bugs are living in the tangles.

The boy in my dream has dirt covering his face, wears a necklace made of animal teeth, and is naked except for an animal hide around his waist. I wonder if he's collected the teeth right off the animal because he has scars on his chest like he had to fight an enormous cat to get them. He's looking at me like I'm strange, too: a modern version of himself in boxer shorts.

Whatever is happening, I'm convinced it isn't real. Since when do dreams come and hang out in your room?

I laugh to myself. What will Dex say about this one? He thinks my imagination is in overdrive as it is. Dex is my best friend. We used to hang out in diapers together. We have photographs to prove it, which we've hidden and hope nobody ever finds.

I wait for the dream to fade. I hum to myself while I wait. To prove the dream isn't real, I reach out to touch the cave boy, expecting him to vanish. But what I touch is a real shoulder. In fact, it's hard as a rock. This kid has serious muscles. He shows his very real teeth and growls at me.

"Whoa!" I say. Then add a few words that could get me grounded for a year.

I jump out of bed and land on my feet. At the same time the cave boy jumps up toward the window.

"This isn't a dream at all," I say to myself.

Coltrane barks like he does when the UPS delivers a package to the door. But this is the strangest package I've ever received, delivered priority mail from a dream into my *real* world.

"What's going on?" I ask. I don't know whether to be excited or terrified. I make Coltrane stop barking because the cave boy is starting to bark back.

Coltrane cowers. For part-bulldog but mostly mutt, he acts tough, but isn't.

The cave boy grunts. He stands on my bed like he's about to pounce on me and wrestle me to the ground. I flash back to Brad Blankenship pushing me off the swing in second grade because he thought I stole his bubble gum. I was so scared I peed a little in my pants. I cross my legs so history won't repeat itself.

The stranger across from me growls and shows his teeth again. Coltrane hides under the bed like he does when Mom wants to give him a bath.

"Hey, calm down. Nobody's going to hurt you," I say to the cave boy, though my first instinct is to run like mad. But this kid could outrun me in a heartbeat. Besides, I'm not the type of guy that wins fights, especially against some kind of prehistoric enemy.

The cave boy growls again. I back up further against my wall, which isn't that easy to do with your legs crossed.

"I'm harmless. I swear," I say. I wonder if he's always this grouchy when he wakes up in the morning.

He grunts again.

I figure out that the grunts are like words, and I'm supposed to know what they mean.

"How'd you get here?" I ask. I talk slow and loud like those bad movies where earth people try to talk to aliens. "Do. You. Know. Where. You. Are? Where. Did. You. Come. From?"

He snarls at me like *The Voice* does when I ask too many questions.

Where's Dad when I need him? I remember how far it is from Atlanta to Oregon and snarl, too. I've been deserted at the worst possible time.

"Okay, okay. We can figure out how you got here later," I say. I take a deep breath to relax so maybe my brain will unfreeze, and I'll know what to do. No such luck.

"This is not a dream," I repeat to myself.

The cave boy scratches his head. Several prehistoric insects fall from his hair and onto my bed before scurrying away under my sheets. Coltrane snaps at one of them on the floor, but it gets away.

"And Mom thinks *my* hair's a mess," I say and manage a smile.

"Mess," he repeats back to me.

My mouth drops open. Did this guy just speak to me? Coltrane sniffs in the direction of our guest. "You can talk?" I ask the cave boy.

"Talk," he grunts back.

I guess they speak English where he's from. Or maybe dream people who become real always speak your language. If some guy in Africa had the same thing happen, the cave boy might be talking in Swahili. But either way, my English teacher wouldn't be too thrilled with his grammar.

"This is unbelievable," I say.

"Unbelievable," he repeats, stumbling over the syllables.

The cave boy and I keep staring at each other, like our brains have short-circuited, and we need time to get used to the idea. But I'm starting to think there's something about this kid I like.

"How'd you get here?" I ask him.

He shrugs—the universal kid gesture for 'I don't know.'

"Do you know how to get back?" I ask.

"Get back?" He shrugs again.

He's a lot smarter than I imagined a cave boy would be. I love reading about history. My room is full of history books. But having a genuine cave boy in my room is way better than reading a book.

"This kind of thing is not supposed to happen," I say. "Never."

"Never," he repeats.

My brain is working way more than usual to figure this out. Maybe the cave boy was dreaming about me at the same time I was dreaming about him and it created an opening, like a black hole or something. Except it's a dream hole, where dreams travel back and forth in time and visit real life. It could happen, right?

I've always had really vivid dreams, anyway. My Grandma Betty says it's because we have Hungarian gypsy blood in our ancestry from seven generations back. Once I dreamed a shark was chasing me and when I woke up I was totally wet and I found a shark tooth in my Batman slipper. Another time I dreamed I was pitching for the World Series and I woke up with a ball glove on my hand. Granted, a cave boy isn't the same as a ball glove, but still.

"Quentin, are you up yet?" *The Voice* yells.

The cave boy jumps like he's heard a ghost. Our eyes reflect panic. Coltrane whines.

"Quentin, if I have to tell you one more time, I'm coming up there!" *The Voice* sounds serious.

At that moment it's like I know his thoughts and he knows mine. A mom showing up—present or prehistoric—is the last thing we need.

"What are we going to do?" I ask the cave boy.

His eyes case the room for an escape.

Mom only comes into my room when she has to; she says the mess in here is toxic to human beings. I hate to think what she'd do if she found a dirt-covered cave boy with bugs in his hair stinking up my already stinky room. Not to mention that I get in trouble if I don't ask her before friends come over, and I'm guessing that means friends from another time period, too.

Footsteps ascend the stairs of our small, two-story house in the suburbs outside Atlanta. The cave boy and I look at each other like a Tyrannosaurus Rex is stalking us for lunch. Coltrane dives under the bed.

"Hide!" My whisper has urgency in it.

We leap in different directions at the same time. The door to my room opens. The cave boy jumps behind it. He's standing inches away from my mom, but out of sight. If he breathes too heavy, grunts, or growls he'll be discovered. And there's no telling how Mom will react. But I'm pretty sure it will involve screaming, calling 911, and dialing an exterminator for the bugs.

"Hi, Mom," I say. Ever since I had a growth spurt over the summer, we stand eye to eye. She's all of 5 feet, 2 inches tall, but her voice is 6'4. I wave my hands like I'm steering small airplanes into their hangars in order to distract her. She looks at me like she's not sure whether to call the pediatrician or Homeland Security. "I told you I was up," I add. I smile and turn on the charm she says the Moss men are famous for.

She sniffs and wrinkles her nose. "It smells like something died in here," *The Voice* says. She turns over a shirt on the floor with the toe of her shoe.

"Dirty clothes," I confess. A visible pile of filthy clothes, about waist high, fills the closet. But what she's really getting a whiff of is prehistoric boy.

"No television until those get done," *The Voice* says. "Come on, Dog," she motions to Coltrane. "Time for your breakfast."

Coltrane whimpers, crawls out from under the bed, and follows her. Mom and Coltrane haven't gotten along since he ate kitty poop from Mrs. Zimmer's flower beds and then jumped into Mom's lap and licked her in the mouth. *The Voice* takes poop personally.

"See you later," I say to Coltrane. I know how he feels. Mom's never forgiven me for the time I discovered that if you shellac dust bunnies with hair spray and run over them with roller blades, they can ignite.

One last time, *The Voice* surveys my room before telling me to get dressed and come to breakfast. Then *The Voice* leaves the room.

As soon as she's gone, the cave boy staggers into the center of the room and we both exhale, like we've been holding our breath for the underwater world record.

"That was close," I say.

"Close," he says back to me. He breathes heavy, as if he's escaped the jaws of a saber-toothed tiger.

"What are we going to do with you?" I ask.

He scratches his head and looks as bewildered as I feel.

Getting him back to where he came from is like trying to get toothpaste back into the tube. Not that he's ever used toothpaste a day in his life from the looks of his mouth. I guess they didn't have dentists back in prehistoric days.

"You can't stay here. We've got to get you home," I say.

"Home," he repeats, like he's already a little homesick.

I look at the clock. I don't have time to figure it out now, or I'll be late to school.

"Mom works at home so you can't stay here," I say to him. "And I'm pretty sure she snoops in my room when I'm gone."

"Snoops," he repeats. He looks at the door.

"I guess you'll have to come to school with me," I say.

"School," he says with confidence, but I can tell he doesn't have a clue what *school* is. If he did, he'd be running as fast as he could back to the Stone Age.

"I guess it can't be worse than what you're used to," I say.

I notice the scars on his chest again and think how middle school can leave scars, too, except ones you can't see. Your parents getting divorced can leave them, too. That's when *The Voice* was born. Plus, your dad leaving home is like getting socked in the gut hard enough that you never want to eat a blueberry pancake again.

I glance over at my new prehistoric friend. If you want to survive, the first rule of middle school is to fit in, and this dude doesn't even begin to.

"First things first," I say. "You need a shower!"

The cave boy grunts and shakes his head no, as if taking a shower is the last thing he wants to do. As we look each other in the eyes, I understand his resistance completely.

Nature Calls

From my bedroom door I look to see if the coast is clear. Then I sneak the cave boy down the hallway and into the bathroom. As soon as I close the door and turn on the light, he freaks and jumps up onto the toilet seat shielding his eyes as if four tiny suns have just appeared in his orbit. I've never seen anybody jump that high and that fast. But I guess you have to be quick if you live in a cave and wild animals want to eat you for lunch.

"It's only a light," I say. "See?" I flip it on and off a few times to show him how it works.

He cowers as if Thomas Edison had invented a total eclipse of the sun instead of a light bulb.

"It's like fire, except better," I say.

He reaches up and touches the decorative bulbs over the mirror. He jumps, then blows on his fingers. "Fire," he says. He snarls at me like I should have warned him.

I realize I'm in for a long day if I have to explain everything invented between the Stone Age and now.

I open the shower curtain and motion for the cave boy to get into the bathtub. He looks at me like I've invited him to step into the arms of a Velociraptor.

"I know the feeling," I say. "But it's only water." After I turn on the water, I splash a handful in his direction. He scrambles behind the toilet and covers his head like I've thrown a hand grenade.

"Relax," I say. "It's only a shower."

His eyes narrow.

"You can trust me," I say. I hold my hand out to him and talk soft like a fireman trying to coax a kitten from a tree. "I hate showers, too," I continue, "but it's something you have to do once you hit middle school or the other kids will make fun of you." I wonder if peer pressure was around in prehistoric times.

The cave boy edges his way closer to the shower. He sniffs the shower curtain, then the handrail and the faucets. I wonder if he's sniffing for danger or mildew. He steps inside the tub, not bothering to take off his animal skin underwear. He's examining the shower nozzle like it's a telescope and he can see the entire solar system from there. When I turn it on he screams. Not a regular scream like girls do if you throw a spider on them, but a primordial one, like something wild is after him and threatening his life. I cover his mouth and he bites me.

"Ouch!" I yelp.

"Quentin, are you all right?" *The Voice* calls from outside the bathroom door. The woman has ears that can pick up the splitting of subatomic particles. She knocks. I lunge for the door, pushing in the lock with my throbbing finger right as she turns the knob. The cave boy's eyes widen. My mom is probably as wild as anything he's ever met in the jungle.

"I'm fine, Mom," I say, trying to sound normal. "The water was really cold."

"You'd think you'd know how to work the shower by now, Quentin," *The Voice* says.

"I know, I know," I say.

"Why did you lock the door?" *The Voice* asks. "I've seen you naked, you know. I used to change your diapers."

"Oh, God, don't remind me," I moan. *The Voice* recites humiliating stories at every opportunity. Her favorites involve diapers, potty seats, and embarrassing body sounds.

"I'm fine, Mom," I say again.

"Hurry up, you need to eat breakfast," *The Voice* says before she walks away. She calls for my sister with a different voice than she uses for me. My sister, Katie, is the princess in our family. I'm the toad. Just ask *The Voice*.

"That was close," I say to my new prehistoric friend.

"Close," he says.

I examine the teeth imprints on my bitten finger. After a few seconds the throbbing starts to go away. At least he didn't break the skin. I'd have a hard time explaining human bite marks in the emergency room.

In the shower, the cave boy takes a bite out of a bar of soap. He spits it out and makes a face like he just ate Brussels sprouts for the first time. I'm not sure but I think one of his teeth came out with it because something hard clangs against the tub.

"No, you use it to clean with," I say. I grab the soap away from him and show him how it works by pretending to wash myself.

"To clean with," he echoes, and sputters out more pieces of soap.

The amount of dirt pouring down the drain could fill a dump truck. In the meantime, I'm envious that he hasn't had to take a shower in his whole life until now. Mom makes me take one every day. If I don't, she threatens to turn the garden hose on me.

I'm showing the cave boy how to use the shampoo when there's a knock at the door. "Hey shrimp, get out of there," Katie calls.

My new friend peeks out from behind the shower curtain. His hair is full of suds. I signal for him to be quiet.

"Just a minute," I say to my sister, like I'm the sweetest little brother on earth.

She pauses. "Hey, why are you being so nice?" she says through the door. I can almost hear her eyes narrow.

"No reason," I say. Niceness is always suspect between us.

"Come on, Q-Tip, let me in." Katie calls me Q-Tip whenever she's trying to get what she wants. Since my hair is blond and kind-of curly she likes to rub the top of my head when she says it.

"I don't look anything like a Q-Tip, you swab."

Katie thumps the door with her claws. "I'm going to tell Mom," she says, which she knows will get a reaction out of me. She inhales, ready to blast the neighborhood with her latest complaint.

"Wait, wait!" I insist. "I'll be right out. Just go to your room or something."

"Why, Q-Tip boy, are you in your birthday suit?"

"Yeah, that's it, Katie," I say. "Now get out of the hall so I can go to my room."

"Quentin's in his birthday suit . . . .," she begins. But at least the taunting is coming from her room.

"We've got to make a run for it," I say to the cave boy.

He's drying off on the first towel he's ever used in his life. He rubs it against his face and sniffs it like he's in a commercial for fabric softener. He refuses to put it down. Even clean, his hair looks wild. I try to brush it before we leave, and he growls at me. I hand him the brush and show him how to do it himself. For several seconds we get nowhere. He has a decade's worth of knots in his hair. With each attempt his growl gets louder.

"Maybe you should pull it back," I say. I hand him one of my sister's hair bands that are always all over the bathroom. "Lots of guys do that these days. Here, I'll show you."

I bunch his hair up into the rubber band.

He makes a face at me like: *you've got to be kidding me.*

"It's the only way," I say. "If we're lucky, people will think you've got dreadlocks."

"Dreadlocks?" he stutters.

"Never mind," I say. Some things are too hard to explain.

He's not too thrilled with the hair thing, but goes along with it.

Opening the door, I check again to make sure the Sister and *The Voice* aren't around. Then I pull the visiting cave boy down the hallway. Once we're inside I latch my bedroom door and throw him some clean clothes from my dresser drawer.

"Here, put these on," I say.

He looks at them, one eyebrow raised.

"Okay, I'll help," I say.

After pulling the T-shirt over his head, I make him change out of his animal skin into a clean pair of my boxer shorts. Then I conceal his smelly hide in the bottom of the clothes hamper. Even covered with clothes, the hamper smells like a combination of wet dog and dead skunk.

"You can't wear the necklace," I say. I point to the collection of teeth hanging around his neck. "It'll draw too much attention. People will think you're in a gang or something." But even in Atlanta I haven't heard of gangs this rough. Some of the teeth look human.

He takes off the necklace made of vine and wrapped carnivore teeth and puts it on the bed. Then I show him how to put the blue jeans on and zip them up. His feet miss the legs several times. But then he secures them around his waist. He studies the zipper, like it's the greatest invention made by mankind, and then slides it up and down about a hundred times.

"Hey, you'd better not do that in public," I say. "The police will come after you."

"Police?" he asks.

"Grownups that carry clubs," I say. "They make everybody follow the rules."

"Clubs," he says. He grunts like he understands and then lets the zipper go. Then he tugs on the seat of his jeans, looking stiff and miserable like I do when I have to wear a suit.

"It'll get better," I say.

His look says: *Yeah, right.*

"Hey, do you have a name?" I ask.

He shrugs, tugs at the seat of his pants a few more times, and then gives the zipper several swift zips.

I decide to show him how greetings in this country are done. I extend my hand. "My name's Quentin. Quentin Moss."

He looks at my hand like there may be a weapon attached. "Moss," he echoes.

I try to explain to him that my name isn't Moss, but Quentin.

"Moss," he repeats.

"Oh, do you like the name Moss?" I ask, figuring I have to call him something.

"Moss," he repeats, as if he's trying it on and it fits fine.

"Moss, it is," I say. "And if anybody asks, you can be my cousin from out of town."

He grunts.

It dawns on me—in a painful way—that while I was so busy hiding Moss I forgot to go to the bathroom. "Wait here," I say.

"Here," he repeats and sits on the bed. He gives his shirt collar a tug. I'm grateful it doesn't have zippers.

From the corner of the bathroom mirror, Katie sees me coming and narrows her eyes. I halfway expect fire to flare out of her nostrils igniting the ton of make-up she's putting on.

"Mom told you not to wear that stuff," I say.

"Get out of here," she says.

"I've got to go to the bathroom, Spazz," I say back at her. Spazz is another one of my pet names for her. I hold the front of my boxer shorts to show how serious I am.

"Why didn't you go while you were in here? And don't call me Spazz, Creep."

"Don't call me Creep, Spazz," I answer back. I imitate her whiny voice, which now that I think about it, sounds a little like Mom's.

"Make this Neanderthal get out of the bathroom!" Katie yells to Mom.

"You have no idea," I say under my breath.

"Quentin, leave your sister alone," *The Voice* says behind me.

I jump like somebody shot me in the behind with a sling shot.

"You're jumpy today, Quentin. Are you okay?" *The Voice* almost sounds nice.

"You keep sneaking up on me," I say. It's a lame comment but maybe she'll believe it. I'm also hoping that she doesn't decide to go into my room where she will find a cave boy named Moss who is a few thousand years old and wearing my clothes. I'll be grounded into the next century.

"Mom, I've got to go," I say. I plant a pained expression on my face, which is only a slight exaggeration of how I feel.

Emergency bodily functions get first priority when three people share a bathroom—especially if one of them is a guy. All I have to do is threaten to go outside in the backyard to relieve myself and it freaks her out. When I was three-years old some older kid told me that peeing on the shrubs was how you watered the lawn. It wasn't until our elderly neighbor complained that I found out that's what garden hoses are for.

I look in the direction of the backyard as a warning.

"Don't you dare!" *The Voice* says. "Katie, your brother needs the bathroom."

"Mom ..." Katie moans.

Mom gives Katie *The Look*, almost always reserved for me, that says *don't mess with me*. After you live with people a long time you can skip the words. All Mom has to do is look at us and we know what she means. *The Voice* and *The Look* are like Siamese twins. Recognizing her text message of looks is crucial, since I don't have dad to decipher her moods. It's pure survival, at this point.

With reluctance, Katie steps aside so I can get in the bathroom. As she walks away, I hold up my arms in victory while she snarls in my direction. A minor battle won in the Quentin/Katie wars. A war I have been drafted into simply by being born.

"You should see what a mess he left in the bathroom, Mom. There's dirt everywhere."

She turns around to gloat. I give my sister a look that needs no translation and throw a wet wash rag at her that misses. Tattling is unforgivable. Any peace treaty we might have been working on is now ripped into bits.

"Quentin, I've told you a thousand times to clean up your messes," *The Voice* says, in tandem with *The Look*. "You don't live in a cave, you know."

I smile. No, I don't live in a cave. But I know someone who does. I realize that with Moss in the picture, I'm no longer out-numbered, and it makes up a little for dad being gone.

Mom goes back downstairs. I go into the bathroom and since I know Katie is waiting, I close the door, determined to take the longest, slowest pee in Quentin Moss history. I write out my entire name with urine and even dot the "I." To further waste time, I also take a long, glacial look in the mirror to search for whiskers that might be breaking through the skin any day now. Facial hair is the first step to freedom from *The Voice* and *The Look*. Once I start to shave, I know my days at home are numbered. I open the cabinet and dash on a handful of Dad's leftover aftershave. It smells potent, and for a second

I feel like I might tear up, and not just from the smell, but from missing my dad.

"Mom, he's taking too long," my sister yells from her bedroom.

"You think this is long, just wait," I say under my breath. I glance at my primitive self in the mirror and grunt.

Hiding Places

Some people play sports or read, but my hobby is to think up ways to irritate my sister. As a younger brother, I consider it my duty. Most of what I come up with would get me arrested. Since I don't think my dog Coltrane would take to living in a jail cell, I resist acting on those. So far I've come up with 77 ways to get revenge.

It's not that my sister and I dislike each other. We hate each other with a passion. When I was four she talked me into playing bull fights. She was the matador. I was the bull. She used her red sweater as the cape and before I knew it my bull horns, as well as my bull head, hit the living room wall going full speed. I almost passed out from the blunt force trauma. Not to mention that my head hurt for about a year after that. It not only left a dent in the wall, but a dent in my skull about the size of a quarter. Whenever my feelings for my sister start to soften, all I have to do is touch the scar and I see red.

More than once I've wished for an older brother to look out for me. It occurs to me that Moss could take my sister in a fight any day.

"Mom, get this cretin out of the bathroom," my sister yells, which snaps me out of my fantasy. I remember that Moss is still in my room and listen at the door to make sure I don't hear any grunts or anything.

The Voice yells up the stairs that I've been in the bathroom long enough.

Before leaving, I take action on revenge idea #77 and put a dollop of mom's hemorrhoid cream on Katie's toothbrush so she'll think it's her whitening toothpaste.

"Mom, he's got on that horrible aftershave again," my sister yells, with her own look of revenge.

"Quentin?" *The Voice* yells from the kitchen. "You'd better get breakfast or you're going to be late."

"I'm coming!" I yell back. Yelling is a standard mode of communication in our house since Dad left. My best friend Dex says his family doesn't yell. In fact, they don't even talk to each other. I guess I'd prefer yelling to nothing at all.

The fight with my sister makes me almost forget about the Stone Age kid in my room. I haven't begun to figure out what to do with him. I whistle, hoping something comes to me on the few steps between the bathroom and my room. Whistling always helps me think. But when I walk into my room, I see my problems have only just begun. My window is wide open and there's no cave boy to be seen. I run to the window and hang halfway out to peer into the backyard. There is no exit. The only way to escape is to jump from the second floor window onto an oak tree limb several feet away from the house. I can't imagine how Moss pulled this off without breaking his neck. Something moves in the bushes. I hear a zipper.

"Moss?" I say, in the loudest whisper I can manage.

He looks up at me and smiles as he relieves himself right in the middle of my mom's prize azaleas. I can't tell you how many times I've wanted to do the exact same thing. But while I'm impressed with Moss' resourcefulness and his aim, I imagine the fireworks this will set off with *The Voice* and *The Look* if my mom walks out the back door at this very minute and finds him.

"Stay there!" I say in a loud whisper. I hold up my arm like I've changed into a school crossing guard. Moss finishes watering the azaleas and then flourishes his zipper with impressive speed.

"Don't move!" I insist. I hold out my hand again.

"Don't move!" he repeats, and holds out his hand, too.

I rush to put on my standard middle school outfit—blue jeans, T-shirt, running shoes, and an Atlanta Braves baseball cap that my dad bought me when we went to a ballgame two summers ago. As I'm putting on my socks, I dream up revenge tactic #78, which involves hiding a pair of ripe gym socks under my sister's bed. The smell will be so intense, she'll think there's a corpse buried under her bed in a shallow grave—like Moss smelled when he first arrived.

Revenge may be hereditary. My dad said he used to bug his older sister, too. Sometimes I wish he was still around to give me some pointers. Heather, the waitress he left us for, wears bright red lipstick and chews bubble gum with her mouth open. One Saturday morning, just over a year ago, right in the middle of our father/son time, Dad announced that he and Heather were moving to Oregon to open up their own restaurant. We haven't seen him since. *The Voice* tries not to let me hear her cry, but she does sometimes.

I finish getting dressed and run downstairs to deal with the Stone Age boy in the backyard that has relieved himself all over my mom's blooming pink azaleas.

Moss has given up on the zipper, but is now turning the garden hose on and off, giving the plants a shower, as well as himself. I sneak up behind him in the bushes and grab the hose.

"Put that down, Moss," I say. I'm not too thrilled with how much I sound like *The Voice* and before I can stop myself I also give him *The Look* to show my disapproval.

Unfazed, Moss grunts his usual grunt. Then he starts to sniff like a dog following a scent. His sniffing nose follows a trail that ends up about an inch away from my face. Eyeball to eyeball, he crinkles his nose.

"Animal, dead," he says.

"That's not a dead animal," I say, "that's my aftershave."

"Animal, dead," he says again. He waves his hand in front of his nose to dispel the scent. If a smelly cave boy thinks you stink, that's saying something.

"This stuff grows hair on your face," I say in my defense.

He gives me a look like I'm trying to sell him a used cave with a pack of wild hyenas inside.

"Come on," I say. I motion for him to follow me and lead the way to the tree house, where I can hide him until we leave for school. We sneak from one group of bushes to the next to avoid being seen. The back door opens and we dive into the bushes like Olympic swimmers jumping into the pool at the start of a race. *The Voice* tells Coltrane to go do his business. Coltrane makes a bee-line for us, barking the whole way. *The Voice* yells at him to stop, but then gets distracted and closes the door.

Coltrane joins us under the bush and growls at Moss.

"Stop it, Cole," I say. He looks at me with his big brown dog eyes like he's seeing double. Then he raises his leg and pees right where Moss peed on Mom's azaleas. Dog and cave boy pee glistens on the petals. I roll my eyes. I'm like the only civilized creature here. Considering my own primitive tendencies, that says a lot.

Moss and I crawl from behind the bushes and one of the azalea limbs slaps us hard in the face like it's paying us back for what Moss did. I rub my stinging face and motion for Moss to follow me. At least he's good about going along with what I say. Being in my dream doesn't seem to bother him that much. But my guess is that not all dreams are this easy to deal with. Especially a dream where lions are after you, like the one I had the night before. If a lion had ended up in my bedroom, I might not be here right now. It would have had Quentin pancakes for breakfast.

Once Moss is up the ladder and in the tree house, I relax. Branches almost hide it. "Stay here until I get back," I instruct him.

"Stay here," he repeats. He holds up his arm like he's a school crossing guard again.

"Look at this while I'm gone," I say. I hand him a *National Geographic* Magazine from the pile that used to be my dad's. I open it to a full page picture of a Bengal tiger somewhere in Africa. As soon as he sees it, Moss tosses the magazine to the floor and stomps on top of it like the tiger on the page is dangerous.

"Hey, that tiger's not real," I say. But his eyes are wide like he doesn't believe me.

"See?" I show him a waterfall on the next page.

"Shower?" he asks.

"No, that's not a shower. That's a waterfall."

"Tiger in shower?" His grunt goes up at the end like a question.

"Tiger not real," I say.

"Stay here," I repeat. My mom is going to come looking for me at any minute, I'm sure of it. "Do you understand, Moss? Stay here."

"Stay here," he repeats, not looking up. He flips through the magazine, holding pictures sideways and upside down sniffing and licking the page. He makes a face from the taste. It's the most I've seen anyone ever get out of a *National Geographic.*

Coltrane at my heels, I walk back to the house, passing Mom's azalea bushes on the way, the sun reflecting off the glistening pee. I have to resist adding more to the mix, and I think about how civilized humans have become. In Moss' world, he goes to the bathroom outside all the time. The closest I've ever gotten to that was the one time Mom and Dad took us camping and Dad and I peed out in the woods.

Before going inside I turn around and glance at the hidden tree house that I haven't used in years. Little did I know that it might someday be a hiding place for a prehistoric guest. Dad would be proud of how I've put it to good use again.

On the way inside, it occurs to me that there's something about Moss that I like. Even though he's been transported into a different eon, he's making the best of it. Moss grunts in the distance, and I hear papers being ripped. I can't believe how weird my day has been already, and I haven't even had breakfast yet.

The Stranger

"How's it going, Mom?" I ask, coming in the kitchen door with Coltrane. I realize I sound almost cheerful. Most often, I'm irritable in the morning, especially on school days and especially since Dad left.

The Voice asks what I was doing outside.

"Nothing," I say, hoping she can't hear the racket in the tree house. I sit at the table and pour my cereal, as if everything is normal.

My mom sniffs the air, then opens the refrigerator door and sniffs inside, like she's looking for rotten food. I get *The Look* and she asks if I'm wearing Dad's aftershave again. I say, yes, and *The Voice* has nothing to say back.

Coltrane chomps down on the rest of his breakfast and then walks over to the kitchen table and sniffs in the direction of my face. He sneezes three times in a row and then wipes his snout on my pants.

"Traitor," I say, since it looks like this time he's sided with Mom.

Coltrane whimpers, and I forgive him right away. Just to prove it I let him smell my crotch, which is one of his favorite things to do.

"You're in a good mood this morning," *The Voice* says. She walks over and tries to tame my hair while I eat my Wheaties. I duck away from her touch.

"Can't a guy just be in a good mood?" I ask. I grunt into my cereal.

Mom looks at me like I've turned into a total stranger right in front of her.

A head appears at the kitchen door. At first I panic, thinking Moss has come looking for me, but instead it's Dex, my best bud.

"Hey," he says. He comes in and drops his book bag with a loud thud on the kitchen chair. Dex carries all his school books home with him every night; he's notorious for being over-prepared. He's getting muscles in his arms, though, from lugging all that knowledge around.

"Hey, Dex," I say, pretending to act normal.

Mom hands him the cereal box like he's another one of her kids.

"What's up?" I say. I bite my lip closed, so my excitement about Moss won't blurt out, like diarrhea of the mouth.

"Nothing much," he says. "What's up with you?"

"Nothing much," I answer. It's the biggest lie I've ever told him. What's up is that there's a guy in my tree house who may have seen dinosaurs firsthand. For all I know, he may have one as a pet.

Dex's real name is a huge secret. Hint: It's **not** Dexter. If I ever tell anyone, Dex says that I will live to regret it and I'm not willing to find out what that actually means. All I can say is his parents must have had it out for him from the very beginning. The name Quentin isn't all that great, either. But at least I can use it without kids taking pot shots at me.

If you saw Dex you'd think he was recovering from a freak accident. His hair looks like his finger got stuck in a light socket when he was young. But after seeing Moss, I wonder if it isn't part of his cave boy past. Maybe one of his ancient ancestors saw one saber-toothed tiger too many and his hair stood straight up out of fright and it's lasted all these generations later.

Dex leans across the table and whispers a reminder. This is the morning we're asking Mom about going to the concert this weekend. Since Dex's parents are never around, we need her to drive. Dex's parents work all the time. The good part is that they let Dex do anything he wants, as long as they don't have to take him or pick him up. At times this is a pretty sweet deal. At other times it's total pressure to have that much freedom. I think Dex misses having parents. I know I miss my dad all the time. But being guys, we don't talk about it much.

The one person in my life I never get the chance to miss is my mom. Her office is at home so she's always around, looking out for Katie and me—and Dex. I think my mom sleeps with one eye open since Dad left, just to make sure nothing's happening that she doesn't know about. This is irritating if you're trying to keep something hidden from her—like prehistoric Homo sapiens.

Since I can't tell Dex about Moss with my mom here, the concert is a good diversion. I wonder if Moss can go with us. If a shower head and a zipper excite him, he'll probably flip to see a music concert with all the special lighting, sound equipment, and instruments. Then I wonder if there's somebody in Atlanta who knows how to get Moss back to where he came from. Maybe some scientist or dream expert. But it's hard to imagine anybody believing such a crazy story.

Dex nudges me out of my fantasy.

"Can Dex and I go to a concert this weekend?" I ask my mom.

She pauses, like she's already come up with twenty reasons why it won't work. *The Voice* asks what kind of concert.

"It's a jazz band from New Orleans," Dex answers. "They're almost famous."

My dad has a huge collection of jazz records that he left behind by jazz greats like Charlie Parker, John Coltrane and Miles Davis. Dex and I play them on an old turntable in my basement.

"Where is this concert?" *The Voice* asks me. Since Dex isn't her flesh and blood it's harder for her to say no to him.

"Well, that's the thing, Mom. It's this great group, so they're playing at a club in Underground Atlanta."

The Voice and *The Look* join forces to tell us what a horrible idea this is. It's not safe for kids our age.

"But, Mom . . ."

"I don't think it will work out this time, Quentin."

Dex tugs at his left ear, my signal to shift into phase two of our plans. This stage involves begging and pleading. I also throw in the secret weapon that every kid who wants to manipulate their parents knows—*The Whine.*

The Whine, when used with the correct levels of begging and pleading, is our best chance to get what we want. Whining, of course, is a high-level skill and must be used with caution. Too much and you're irritating. Too little and the target misses. Both will get a negative response.

"Oh, come on, Mom," I say. I insert *The Whine* in millisecond proportions. I imagine Moss using this strategy with his mom in order to visit a distant cave and getting clobbered with a club.

"I don't think this is a good idea," *The Voice* says. Her tone is about as far away from a whine as you can get.

"Don't you remember what it's like to be my age?" I ask. I look her straight in the eyes. Eye contact is another strategy to getting what you want. If anything can get through to my mom it's the big brown eyes that she told me once looked like my dad's. Of course, this might count against me because of the blueberry pancake lady, which is what I call Heather in front of my mom.

"Please, Mom?" I insert *The Whine* again. "Dad would let me."

Dex's eyes widen, like I've pulled the pin out of a hand grenade and the whole thing may blow up in my face. We wait for an explosion, but *The Voice* goes silent and *The Look* drops. Mom pours Dex a second glass of orange juice.

"We could stay for just the first set and you could wait in the car," I say.

The Voice sighs.

"What if Moss goes with us?" I say. "He could be our own personal body guard." Within seconds I realize that I have just let an enormous Stone Age cat out of the bag.

"Moss?" *The Voice* asks.

"Moss?" Dex says.

They both look at me like I've admitted I have an imaginary friend.

I stutter around searching for a response. "I was just saying that if a Moss man can't do it who can?"

Dex drops his head to his chest, like all hope is lost. But I have one more thing to try: our final, final resort, minus *The Whine*.

I begin again, using my most grown up voice. "Mom, you need to remember that in only a few years I'll be twenty. I can handle more responsibility, now."

The plan is to project myself into the future, and have my mom imagine me not as her little son, Quentin, but as a mature, twenty-year-old, already in college or off on my own; a person capable of going to a concert in Underground Atlanta without placing my life in any danger.

Dex lifts his head, a glimmer of expectation in his eyes. We wait for *The Voice*.

My mom's face softens. She pours herself another cup of coffee. Then a brief smile comes and goes. The longer she waits to respond, the more hopeful I get. I hear music from the concert play faintly in the background. But then *The Voice* wagers a brilliant counter-attack. "That's a good point, Quentin, but you're also only a few years away from being a five-year-old."

Our hopes deflate in an instant. Good one, *Voice*. TKO.

Both things are true. Some days I am very mature: a twelve, going on thirteen-year-old Dalai Lama in training, ready to scale the Himalayas. Other days I trip over my shoe laces and squirt apple juice out of my nose.

I can't imagine Moss having problems like this. When you're one of the original boys, I think life must come down to basics: surviving a cold winter, getting through your child-hood without getting eaten by a bear or falling off a cliff, or avoiding a disease that today that can be cured with an aspirin.

As for me, life has changed pretty fast. One minute I'm bored to death, and the next minute I've got a visitor from the Stone Age in my tree house. Before this morning it seemed like all the interesting things happen to somebody else. But now I'm that somebody. The only downside is that now that something this amazing has happened, I can't tell anyone. Except Dex. If I can trust anyone, it's the friend that I've had since we both wore Huggies.

The School Bus

Dex and I finish breakfast and grab our book bags. Before we leave, Mom leans in to kiss me. I dodge away from her and she kisses the air instead. *The Voice* calls after us to have a good day. Dex and I go out the back door toward the bus stop. As soon as we get around the corner of the house, I pull him near the bushes so I can tell him about Moss. Since Dex isn't used to being jerked around he looks surprised.

"Hey, what's up?" Dex says.

"I'd be careful where I step if I were you," I say, looking around at where Moss had been.

He looks at me like I've morphed into a hobbit and I'm lost somewhere between here and Middle Earth. "You're acting strange this morning," Dex says. "Did you get a call from your dad or something?"

"Even better," I say. For the first time this morning I let out my excitement and it's like my legs have springs. I can't stay still.

"Quentin, what's going on?" Dex asks.

"The strangest thing happened this morning, Dex, I mean really strange."

"Tell me," he says. He puts his book bag on the ground like this may take a while. "But you'd better hurry or we'll miss the bus."

"You know the bus is always late," I say.

"What is it?" he asks again.

"I was sleeping, you know, and then I was dreaming, and then the dream kind of became real."

"Yeah, right," Dex says, like this is the millionth time I've pulled his leg and he's not going to fall for it again.

"I'm telling you the dream became real." I look at him like I'm the most serious I've ever been in all the years he's known me.

"How can a dream become real? I don't get it," he says, once he realizes I'm not playing a joke on him. Dex isn't the most excitable human being on the planet. It's like he owns the patent to staying calm.

"I was having this dream about this kid in a cave. He was our age, but he was a *cave* kid, and there was this cave mom trying to get him up, like my mom was trying to get me up. And then both moms said 'get up' at the same time and suddenly this kid in the dream was on my bed. Like some kind of spell clicked in and transported him from there to here."

"Are you sure that part wasn't a dream, too?" Dex asks.

He isn't getting it. "No, I mean he's actually here."

"Where?" he says, looking around.

"In the tree house," I say back.

"The tree house?"

"Yeah."

"There's a cave boy in the tree house?"

"Yeah."

"Yeah, right." He shakes his head like this is the wildest story he's ever heard.

"I kind of wish I was kidding," I say, "because now I don't know what to do with him. I don't know how to get him back to where he came from."

"Unreal," Dex says.

"You aren't kidding," I say back.

"This is a real weird problem to have."

"Tell me about it," I say.

"How do you know you're not dreaming now?" Dex says.

"I don't know," I say. "Maybe I am."

I pinch Dex and he pinches me. We punch each other in the shoulders and the pain feels very real.

"Grandma Betty says I have vivid dreams because we have Hungarian gypsy blood in our lineage."

"But isn't this the same woman who dresses up her terriers in Zorro costumes?"

Dex has a point. "That's only for Halloween," I say.

Dex pauses like I've outdone my usual crazy. "I need to see this guy," he says finally.

"Okay, but after that we've got to decide what to do with him while we're at school. I was thinking about taking him along. Maybe he could be my cousin or something. A shy cousin who doesn't talk much."

"That could work," says Mister Calm.

What I like about Dex is that if I tell him that aliens have landed in his back yard and I need help greeting them, he'll show up.

When we go into the tree house Moss sits behind a tall stack of torn out pages that are crumpled and wet like he's been licking them.

"Dex, this is Moss. Moss, this is Dex," I say by way of introduction.

Moss does a double take when he sees Dex. I guess Dex isn't the most normal looking human of the 21st century. Meanwhile, Dex is doing a double take, too. He looks kind of pale.

Moss smiles, showing a mouthful of teeth that could use some industrial strength dental floss.

"What do you think?" I ask Dex.

"About what?" Dex stares at Moss like he's trying to decipher a complex math problem.

"What do you think about Moss?"

"His name is Moss?"

"Yeah, but what should I do with him? Do you think he could pass for a kid like us?"

Dex closes his mouth. He circles Moss, as if studying the problem from every angle.

Moss circles, too, as if studying Dex's hair from every angle.

They look like two wrestlers circling each other before they go at each other's throats, but then they both stop.

"He could probably pass," Dex says. "Just tell everybody he's from L.A."

"That might work," I say. California is about as far away and weird as people living in Georgia can imagine. I look at my watch. "We've got to go. If we miss the bus, Mom will have to take us."

We usher Moss down the ladder of the tree house and walk toward the bus stop. Moss walks in the middle, like he's an FBI informant and we're two federal agents escorting him to a courtroom to give expert testimony about what's it's like to come from another epoch.

"Does he talk?" Dex asks, keeping his eyes straight ahead.

"Yeah, a little bit," I say. "But mostly he grunts and growls."

Moss grunts, like he understands every word.

"Amazing," Dex says again.

"Amazing," Moss repeats.

Dex and I look over at each other like this is our best adventure yet. Better than the massive roller coaster at Six Flags Over Georgia that Dex and I rode fifteen times in one day, setting a personal record. We were going for twenty but the attendant asked us to leave because Dex's hair was scaring younger kids.

As we come around the corner to the bus stop, a car beeps its horn and speeds by. Before we know it Moss climbs Mr. Hyatt's maple tree in breakneck speed. All I can see are Moss' eyes peering out between the leaves and they look a little wild, like he's Ebenezer Scrooge and he's seen the ghost of Christmas future.

"I guess he's never seen a car before," Dex says.

"No kidding," I say, putting down my book bag. I try to coax Moss out of the tree because Mr. Hyatt hates kids, especially in his yard, and he might call the police. "Moss, come out of that tree. It was only a car."

"Car?" Moss asks.

For the first time since we met, Moss looks a little scared. I guess a piece of flashy metal speeding by is intimidating if you're from a time when the wheel hasn't even been invented.

"Come on, Moss. I've got your back," I say.

"Got my back?" Moss asks. He glances behind him, then back at me.

"Yes," I say. I feel protective of my new friend. We've all been in uncharted territory before. I wish somebody had been around to show me how to get along without a dad after he left.

Moss climbs out of the tree as fast as he scaled it. He must have learned to climb trees to get away from wild animals. When another car goes by Moss starts to duck and run, but I grab him before he can. I lock my arm in his and reassure him that this is normal stuff and we keep walking. After we get to the bus stop the other kids stare at Moss and whisper. Moss sniffs in their direction like he's on the scent of some real danger.

"Maybe this isn't such a good idea," Dex says, watching their reaction.

"What else are we going to do with him?" I ask. "It's not like he can stay in my room. If Mom finds him she'll end up calling the police or something. Then he'll never get home. It's my fault he's here, Dex. I've got to figure out how to get him back."

Dex nods like he understands. "Any ideas of how to do that?"

"Nope," I say, which is the dead-on truth. I have no idea how to get through the next few minutes, much less a zillion time zones to the Ice Age to return a prehistoric kid to his cave. For about the tenth time this morning I'm wishing Dad was here. Not that he would know what to do, either. But I'm pretty sure his reaction would be better than Mom's.

"I guess for now we have to figure out how to get him in school," Dex asks.

"I have an idea," I say. "I just hope Mr. Richie isn't there today." Mr. Richie is the assistant principal and he doesn't trust anybody. He stands outside the school and watches the students like we're all carrying automatic weapons in our backpacks. I can't imagine him letting a kid he doesn't recognize walk right into the building.

At the bus stop three girls start to giggle because Moss is tugging at the seat of his pants again. I'm praying that he doesn't start with the zipper.

Moss growls and the girls giggle again. Seconds later they decide to give him the royal brush off, which throughout the eons must feel the same, because Moss' growl turns into a prehistoric pout.

"It's hard to be different," I say.

"Tell me about it," Dex says. He takes a photo of Moss with his iPhone.

"Tell me about it," Moss repeats in half-grunts and half-speaks. Moss gets the Nobel Prize for being different.

When the bus arrives we have to drag Moss on. I try to imagine what it's like to hop on a big yellow container with an engine, wheels, and a bunch of strangers. When the driver revs the engine, Moss' eyes widen. We grab his arms so he won't jump off the bus and run for Mr. Hyatt's tree again. It takes several blocks before he settles into his seat.

A stop or two later, Moss starts playing with the latches on the bus windows. He opens and closes them as fast as he can, like he was doing his zipper earlier. The bus driver has her eye on us through the rear-view mirror. Dex and I take turns grabbing Moss' hands to make him stop. But it isn't working.

Finally, Dex sits his heavy backpack in Moss' lap. It's a brilliant idea because Moss stops with the windows and starts zipping and unzipping Dex's backpack a zillion times. The bus driver quits giving us the evil eye. When we approach the school I realize our adventure has only just begun.

Prison Time

By the time the bus pulls up to the front of our middle school, my stomach feels queasy, and not because I'm about to take a cave boy into my school. Queasiness is my usual reaction to this place. I grip my backpack and feel like a prisoner arriving at San Quentin Prison to do hard time. My task for the next seven hours is to get out of this place alive.

After taking a deep breath, I get off the bus. The crowd is thick. Within seconds I realize Moss isn't with me. When I look back I see him playing with the bus door. Silver lever in hand, Moss opens and closes the door with a satisfied grin. Meanwhile, the bus driver is threatening to take him to the principal's office.

I grab Moss' hand off the lever and apologize to the bus driver. "He's from California," I say.

She raises an eyebrow like she understands. "Well, if he tries that again he can't ride this bus anymore," she says, as tough as any prison guard when it comes to her bus.

I apologize again. Like a parent pulling a kid out of the cereal aisle at a grocery store, I pull Moss toward the gray building. We follow the flow of human traffic. Moss tugs at the seat of his pants again and grunts loudly. A few people stop to stare.

"Good luck," Dex says, as we approach the front doors. This is where we split off every morning and go to homeroom.

"Thanks," I say. My stomach lurches when we go inside, and I try not to toss my Wheaties. At best, middle school is like a zombie movie that you can't stop watching even though you're scared to death. It's not for the squeamish. Even if you're one of the popular kids, your fate can change in an instant.

"See you after first period," Dex calls after me.

"If I live that long," I call back.

I take Moss by the arm and go into the office. The good news: Assistant Principal Richie is nowhere in sight.

"This may actually work," I say to Moss. We stand at the front desk to sign him in as a visitor. My shoulders relax, and then a *Big Voice* booms behind me, like someone talking through a bullhorn.

"And who is this?" *Big Voice* asks.

I turn around. Principal Proctor eyes Moss with suspicion. His voice is the biggest thing about him, and compared to Mr. Richie he's a pushover. But my palms are leaking sweat anyway.

"Hello, Mr. P-Proctor, this is my c-cousin," I begin. "He's v-visiting from California." My mom says I'm not a very good liar because it's the only time I stutter.

"I didn't know you had family in California, Quentin," *Big Voice* says.

"My dad's side," I say.

He nods his head like what I've said is now believable.

A few months after my dad left, Mr. Proctor had two dates with my mom. They met on an online dating service. Luckily, *The Voice* from home and *Big Voice* from school didn't hit it off. Otherwise I may have been forced to run away from home just to get some quiet. It also means I don't have to worry about Mr. Proctor calling my mom to check out the California story. But he still treats me like the son he almost had.

"Welcome to Franklin Middle School," *Big Voice* says to Moss. He hands him a special visitor's pass. Before we walk away he pats Moss on the back. I grab Moss' arm, right as he's about to throw Mr. Proctor to the ground.

"My cousin isn't comfortable with strangers touching him," I say. I smile like the son he might have had and Moss and I get out of the office before anybody gets hurt.

In the hallway, an eighth grader walks by with dyed green hair and his nose pierced in three different places. Moss breaks into a laugh. It's the first time I've heard him laugh and it wouldn't be bad, except it sounds like a very large, very loud goose doing a mating call. In a matter of seconds he's drawn another crowd.

I pull Moss into the boy's bathroom as fast as I can. Two boys leave in a hurry because Moss can't stop honking. "Quiet," I warn him.

"Quiet," he repeats, still honking away. I flush a toilet to get his attention. He stops honking to watch the water swirl and go down the bowl. I stop him from putting his head in there to see where the water went. When new water fills the bowl his face lights up like it's Christmas morning.

"Fire?" he asks.

He must be remembering the light bulb from this morning. "No, it's water," I say.

He nods. "Water," he repeats.

The first bell rings and Moss jumps onto the sink like a herd of elephants are charging him. I reassure him that we're safe. We leave the bathroom and step back into the flow of traffic. Moss sniffs random people; their back packs, their clothes. Some laugh. Some push him away. Some ignore him. He's fitting right in.

At my locker I get out my biology book that I'll need right after homeroom and hand it to Moss. "Hold that for me," I say.

He grunts, takes the book, and starts flipping through it. For someone who doesn't read he really likes magazines and books. He's about to tear out a picture of a magnified amoeba, but I grab his hand. "Don't destroy school property," I say.

"Don't destroy," he repeats. He looks disappointed.

"And don't grunt or growl about anything, either. And don't laugh."

"Don't laugh," he says with a frown. I didn't realize until now how many rules kids have to live by just to stay out of trouble. Moss acts like he understands. He stops sniffing and imitates the way I walk and hold my head. It's all about fooling people into thinking you're cool, even when you're not. Instinctively, Moss knows he's different, and different can be dangerous.

My homeroom teacher, Mr. Baxter is counting the days until he retires. A big, red 178 is written in the corner of the dry erase board. Tomorrow there will be a 177. As long as we don't kill anybody in homeroom, he leaves us alone. He doesn't even take role any more.

When the announcements come on Moss jumps and stares at the ceiling like enemy invaders are coming through the roof. A couple of guys elbow each other and laugh, but nobody else notices. Everybody is half-asleep for homeroom anyway or trying to finish homework that's due later in the day. Announcements end and Moss relaxes. Then the bell for first period rings and he crouches behind a desk as student's spring toward the door. His survival instincts are good and will come in handy for the next few hours.

We enter first period, biology class, and the smell of formaldehyde almost knocks us over. Today is the day we're going to dissect frogs. Some of the girls are already squealing in disgust at the idea of making the first slice. Moss imitates their squeals, and I poke him in the ribs. He grunts and pokes me back. I squeal like one of the girls, too, because it hurts.

Miss Joyce, my biology teacher, stands by the door and hands us each a small cutting tool sealed in plastic. "Who's this?" Miss Joyce asks, looking at Moss.

"My cousin," I say. "He's visiting from California."

Miss Joyce smiles. "What part of California?" she asks.

Moss looks at me and grunts a question mark.

"Oh, uh, he's, uh, from Hollywood," I say. "His agent is trying to get him in a remake of the movie, Encino Man."

Miss Joyce doesn't even blink and congratulates Moss on his acting career.

Speaking of Hollywood, Miss Joyce could easily be the Wicked Witch of the West's younger sister from *The Wizard of Oz*. Her nose is pointed and she wears black a lot. Even though it's ancient, my family used to watch the movie, *The Wizard of Oz*, together every Halloween. It's my mom's favorite. One year at Halloween my dad dressed up as one of the flying monkeys. He scared little kids when he was handing out candy at our door so Mom didn't let him do it again. She said he could be the wizard behind the curtain but not in public. I prefer *Oz the Great and Powerful* myself.

If I dressed up as a character right now I would either be the scarecrow without a brain or the cowardly lion. For one thing, I can't think up how to get Moss back to where he came from. And also I'm scared to death that someone will find out our secret and take him away to wherever prehistoric juveniles are detained. I could use a wizard behind the curtain right now. But he seems to have taken up residence in Oregon with Glinda, the gum-chewing witch.

"Can Moss and I be lab partners?" I ask Miss Joyce.

"Certainly," she says.

Miss Joyce is permanently laid back; nothing seems to bother her. If she found out about Moss I could probably talk her into not telling.

I lead Moss to the container of formaldehyde and use tongs to pick out the biggest frog corpse I can find and put it on a little tray. Moss sticks his nose in the container and sniffs deeply. As a result, he starts to cough, which sounds a lot like his laugh. Then he falls backward from the smell of the chemicals.

"What are you doing?" I whisper. I pull him over to the lab table. He shrugs and sits on the stool in front of the frog body on the tray. Formaldehyde can preserve things for years. For all we know this frog could be leftover from cave men times.

While we're waiting Moss begins to look at the frog like he's considering it for a snack. He picks it up by one of its petrified legs.

"No!" I say. I knock the frog out of his hand right before he's about to take a bite. For the first time I realize the guy must be starving because he didn't have anything for breakfast. It never entered my mind that a dream image might need to be fed. I rummage around in my back pack and find half of a petrified peanut butter and jelly sandwich left over from the week before.

"Here, eat this," I say. Before I can stop him he starts eating the whole thing, including the zip-lock bag.

"Wait!" I say. "Take off the plastic first." I grab it back and pull off the plastic which is now covered with teeth marks and saliva. I feel like I'm babysitting a two-year-old. Moss doesn't know anything.

Hannah and Haley, the girls at the lab table behind us, start to whisper. They are cheerleaders and two of the most popular girls in school. Moss is oblivious to social status and the fact that guys like us are never supposed to approach or acknowledge girls like them. He turns to face them and crams the whole sandwich in his mouth at once. He gags before swallowing it whole.

"Gross!" Hannah and Haley say in unison.

"He's from California," I say to them.

Moss belches a cave size belch and smiles, revealing pieces of leftover plastic bag sticking between his teeth.

Meanwhile, Moss begins to forage for more food. He eyes a collection of roots and berries from the botany section in the back of the room.

"I'll get you more food after class," I say, hoping he can wait that long. I wish our science department had a time machine or a space shuttle or something, anything to get Moss back home.

Our tiny glassy-eyed victim stares up from the lab table in front of us. In order to get credit, we have to cut our frog open with a scalpel, stretch him apart with pins, and then identify his internal organs. I study the diagram of how we're supposed to do it. When Miss Joyce gives the go-ahead, I make the first slice. The skin makes a popping noise as it opens. A disgusting smell escapes from under the skin. Suddenly, the room gets hot and starts to spin. I feel like I'm going to pass out in a heap on the gray tile floor. I grab the table, handing the scalpel to Moss.

"You've got to do it," I say, nodding toward the frog.

Moss looks at the scalpel and studies the blade. He looks like something like this could come in handy where he's from. Then he steps up to the frog and deftly peels off the skin to expose the muscle, like he's done it a thousand times before. He isn't grossed out at all. I'm already counting on this being the first $A+$ I'll ever get in biology when Moss cuts out the frog's tiny intestines and flings them over his shoulder in the direction of Hannah and Haley.

They let out a blood-curdling, eardrum-ripping scream. Miss Joyce runs to the back of the room. After the girls calm down, Miss Joyce gives me a look like my flying monkey days are over. On behalf of Moss and me, I apologize to both girls and Miss Joyce.

The truth is Moss is doing things I wish I had the guts to do. Before our lab time is over, he tosses the little frog brain in Hannah's direction, too. And for his grand finale he pops both frog eyes out of the sockets and tosses them into Haley's lap. She runs out of the room, her hands covering her mouth, like she's about to lose her breakfast. Two slimy frog eyes stick to her white skirt, and look back at me and Moss as she flees.

I've never been so grossed out in my life, but it's also the most fun I've ever had in biology. In that moment I decide that if Moss gets stuck in the 21st century and ever becomes a surgeon, he's never getting his hands on me. Despite this fact, I'm in awe of the damage that can be done to a frog using a scalpel and a little imagination. There isn't much left of the poor amphibian by the end of the period.

"Another life donated to science," I say to Moss.

"Huh?" he grunts back.

"Never mind," I say.

Even though she's probably dissected millions of frogs, when Miss Joyce sees Moss's work she turns a shade of green I've never seen before. At that moment all she needed was a little theatrical make-up and a pointed black hat, and she could easily get a part in a remake of *The Wizard of Oz* and give up teaching all together.

As for the frog:

> May he
> rest in
> pieces.

Go, Tigers!

"How's it going?" Dex asks in the hallway between classes.

"I think a convicted felon could be brought into this place as long as he kept quiet," I say. "The only thing middle school teachers care about is whether a person can keep their mouth shut or not."

"I hear you," Dex says. "How'd he do in biology?"

"Don't even ask," I say. "Hey, do you have anything that he can eat? I forgot to feed Moss this morning."

Dex digs around in his backpack and produces a strawberry fruit roll-up. I take off the wrapper and hand it to Moss who swallows it in one gulp. The bell rings for second period and Dex gives me a thumbs up for good luck and takes off. But I'll need more than a thumb for luck in Mr. Griffin's English class. We don't have assigned seats, so I choose two desks near the back of the room in case Moss grunts, growls or sniffs.

Mr. Griffin, also known as Mr. G, is one of those teachers who thinks it's his job to mold young minds. He's actually used those very words. I always think of the molds that come with the play dough factory. If he could mold my mind into a pink giraffe or a yellow elephant I think that would be pretty cool. But otherwise, it seems like a lost cause.

"Quentin, would you like to introduce your friend to us?" Mr. G. says after everyone is seated.

I stand, looking nervously at Moss. I hope he doesn't pick this moment to start playing with his zipper or tugging at the seat of his pants.

"This is Moss," I say to the class. "He's my cousin from California." I pull Moss up by the elbow. We stand side by side looking like two mug shots of the ten most wanted criminals.

"Welcome, Moss," Mr. G. says. "Why don't you tell us something about your school in California?"

A prickly panic rises up the entire length of my body. Moss looks at me to see what to do. "He doesn't talk much," I say for him. "He's really shy."

"That's fine, just tell me one thing you like about your school," Mr. G. says to Moss, like he's willing to mold a mind from California, too.

Everybody in the class turns around to look at Moss. My flight reflex kicks in and I look for an exit. Moss nudges me, like he's the one telling *me* to stay calm. Predators love it when prey runs. My heart beats faster than normal and I imagine the worst: Moss grunts and jumps on top of one of the desks, then plays with his zipper before taking a leak all over everybody. I'll get the fastest expulsion in middle school history. As a result, I'll have to be home-schooled and listen to *The Voice* all day, every day for the rest of my life! I tug at my shirt collar and feel enough sweat in my pits to fill an Olympic-sized pool.

"Tigers," Moss says finally.

"Your football team is called the tigers?" Mr. G. asks.

"Tigers," Moss repeats. He looks pleased with himself. I grab his hand right before he grabs his zipper.

"Go, Tigers!" I say, shaking imaginary pom-poms. I pull Moss down into the chair and breathe the longest sigh of relief in the history of close calls. Unfortunately, Moss' jungle sweat glands have clicked in big time and I wish I'd thought to make him put on deodorant this morning. He smells like an overripe dumpster. In this school, if you smell bad you're thrown to the wolves. For the first time I understand what that phrase really means. Where he's from, getting thrown to the wolves means *real* wolves.

"That was close," I whisper to Moss.

"Close," Moss says, wiping the sweat from his forehead.

The guys on the back row, who are gang members in training, cover their noses with their hoodies, but they don't look willing to say anything to Moss about how he smells.

"Get out your journals," Mr. G. tells the class. Everyone moans. Mr. G. is real big on journals. He's kept one since he was a kid. I've never known a teacher to admit to being totally uncool. But he honestly believes it's a way to get to know yourself, which he says isn't an easy task for people our age.

In a way Moss seems more real than anybody here. Even though he doesn't know how to read or write—in his world schools and books haven't been dreamed up yet—he's smart. I hand him an encyclopedia from the back of the room and he's captivated again. He thumbs through the pages, looking at all the pictures. He starts to tear one out and I give him *The Look* and he stops.

"Journal writing helps you discover who you are," Mr. G. begins. "At first, your thoughts may seem primitive..."

"Is he serious?" I whisper to Moss. "He has no idea what primitive is."

Moss grunts loudly. People pivot in our direction.

To draw them off his scent, I begin to cough like a peanut the size of New Hampshire is stuck in my windpipe.

"Quentin, do you need some water?" Mr. G. asks.

"No. Thanks." With a few more coughs I end my performance. The whole class looks a little disappointed that I've recovered. If I had choked to death they might have gotten out of class early. Since I already have everybody's attention, I decide to speak up.

"Mr. G., you make it sound like if we journal we're going to uncover some kind of cave man part of ourselves," I say. A few girls give a nervous laugh, like I'm making a total fool of myself and they're glad it's not them.

"Cave people had a need to express themselves, too," Mr. G. says. "Scientists have found cave paintings dating back to prehistoric times."

I look over at Moss. If Mr. G. knew who Moss really was, he'd be writing non-stop in his journal for the next twenty years. Or maybe he'd write a newspaper story about it. He's the advisor for our school newspaper. In my imagination I see headlines: Quentin Moss Finds Primitive Boy.

"What should we write about?" I ask Mr. G. Bravery comes easy when you've already made a fool of yourself.

"Write whatever comes to you, Quentin," he says.

"What if nothing comes to me?" I ask. This draws a laugh, but I wasn't trying to be funny.

"Write like you're talking to a friend," he says. "Write like you're writing to Moss."

The blank page in my spiral notebook matches the blank page in my mind. I'm not alone. The whole class looks like their minds are computer hard drives that have crashed.

"Get started," Mr. G. instructs.

I feel unequipped for the task, like I'm attempting to scale Mt. Everest wearing flip-flops, shorts, and a T-shirt.

Moss is watching me, and I decide to use Mr. G.'s suggestion and write to him to see if it will get me started.

Dear Moss,

I've had a really interesting day so far, thanks to you. Who would have thought that a dream could become real and that a real live cave boy could end up sitting at the end of my bed? I want to thank the black hole of dreams or my Hungarian ancestors.

The writing goes well after that, as I write about the events of the day. After I see what I've written I realize that keeping my thoughts in a notebook instead of keeping them locked

away in my head is risky business. Especially if you've got secrets. Mr. G. has promised not to read a word, but the rest of
the world hasn't made that promise.

I decide if someone finds my journal I could be in big
trouble. Possible consequences, which I write down, include:

(1) Someone calls the news media.

*(2) News reporters show up and start taking photographs of me and
Moss. YouTube videos spring up everywhere. Bloggers in Hungary are
hungry for content.*

*(3) Photographs appear on websites and newspapers all over the
world.*

*(4) Moss is taken away by the government to an underground mili-
tary base in New Mexico and I never see him again.*

*RESULT: I'm a freak of nature—the kid who dreamed up a cave
boy. Eventually, I end up living in a cave myself, just to get away from
the press.*

*In sum, I'll always be remembered as one of the following: a) a hero,
b) a nut case, c) the village idiot, or d) all of the above.*

My imagination dreams up the worst. Before the media
frenzy is over, I'll have my own reality show devoted to un-
covering how a dream crosses over into real life. They'll show
the bed I sleep in, the shower where Moss took his first
shower, the tree house, the middle school. They'll follow my

teachers around and ask them about what kind of student I am, especially the ones that don't like me. They'll have re-en-actments of Moss arriving out of the dream, Moss on the school bus, Moss in biology. . . .

Scientists will hook me up to electrodes to monitor my brain waves while I'm sleeping. I'll never get a good night's sleep again. I might quit dreaming altogether.

Since disaster isn't new to me, I remember one of the worst days of my life that happened last year while sitting on the school bus with Heather Parker during the end-of-the-year field trip. Sitting with somebody on a bus trip means you're serious, and just as I was getting used to the idea of Heather being my first girlfriend, without any explanation, she col-lected all her things and moved to the back of the bus. Every-body on the bus saw it, and I was mortified. Rejection with a capital R, which isn't easy under any circumstances, especially in front of all the other kids. Talk about primitive. In middle school, feeling sorry for a person isn't allowed. Once they see you're weak they start to attack. Heather's friends laughed and made fun of me for the next hundred miles.

Later, I found out Heather Parker liked a guy named Brady more than me and her friends had dared her to sit with me.

Brady Johnson = tall, athletic, good looking, soccer player
Quentin Moss = short, clumsy, average looking, band geek

Afterward, Heather told people that the reason she broke up with me was because my gums showed too much when I laughed. To top it off she said she wouldn't dream of kissing me because it would be like kissing a horse. She compared me to a talking horse on the Cartoon Network called Mr. Ed. Evidently Mr. Ed has buck teeth and gums the size of a small Buick.

Needless to say, being compared to a farm animal is not something someone of any age wants to hear. The humiliation was so complete it felt like it might affect me in later life, too. Like I would never discover a cure for cancer now or win the Nobel Peace Prize. All because Heather Parker didn't have anything to do in the evenings and watched Nickelodeon.

For six months afterward I vowed never to laugh in public again. I refused to show my gums for any reason. I avoided Heather Parker and her friends like they carried the plague. Then one day I went to school and took a good look at Heather. What gave her the right to say those things about me, anyway? She had okay gums but a crooked smile and ears that stuck out. I'd rather be referred to as Mr. Ed than Dumbo.

Since Heather's rejection I've grown up a lot. After months of practice in front of the mirror I've figured out a way to laugh and not show my gums at all. I've also done everything I can to avoid embarrassment. Not that people finding out about Moss would be embarrassing. But it would draw a lot of attention that I don't think either one of us is ready for.

On a blank page of my journal I write:

Red Alert: For security purposes, while at home I'll keep this journal in my closet. Nobody can find anything in there anyway, not even me. While at school, I will NEVER let my journal out of my sight.

The bell rings and scatters my thoughts. I secure my journal in my book bag and look over at Moss, whose eyes are glazed over. For the last twenty minutes he's been watching the second hand of the clock go around. Welcome to my world, Moss, the world of middle school and terminal boredom. He probably never gets bored a day in his life where he's from. I imagine a typical day for him. He attacks a bear with a stone knife, then skins it and wears its fur on a winter day.

"Home?" Moss asks as we get up to leave.

"I wish," I say.

One of those prehistoric pouts starts to form on Moss' face again.

"It'll be over before you know it," I add, sounding like *The Voice* before I got shots at the doctor's office when I was little.

As we leave class Mr. G. smiles at Moss and says, "Go, Tigers!"

Moss grunts, smiling awkwardly.

I tug him toward the door. "Go, tigers!" I repeat.

We join the chaos of students changing classes. When it comes to the chaos of a hundred kids in one hallway going to different places all at the same time, Moss is pretty fearless now. At least he isn't out with a hunting party having to kill a woolly mammoth or something. For all I know this may feel like a vacation to him.

The closest I can imagine to what his life must be like is when my family went on our one and only camping trip. We hiked, swam in the river, and had campfires at night. Of course we slept in a tent instead of a cave and all our food came from a grocery store instead of us having to hunt it down and kill it ourselves. But to us, we were roughing it.

Two classes down with three to go. We've had some close calls already. I'm not sure how we'll make it to three o'clock. Plus, the nightmare of my existence is next: gym.

Survival of the Fittest

Gym class makes no sense. Why get a whole bunch of middle school guys together in one room and run them around until they smell like a landfill on a hot, sunny day?

As usual, the tension in the room is thick as everybody checks out everybody else to make sure the pecking order hasn't changed. I never have to worry about threatening the bigger guys. Since grade school, some of the same guys have been making fun of my legs. They've been called chicken legs, pencil sticks, bean poles. Once somebody even gave me a note that said Colonel Sanders was looking for me. Can I help it that my legs stay as white as the inside of a McNugget, no matter how much I stay outside all summer?

I give Moss my extra pair of gym shorts to wear. He keeps looking for the zipper and looks disappointed that there isn't one. He lines up like everybody else. We all look like weaklings compared to him. His body has scratches and scars all over his arms and legs like he's been living in the big cat cage at the zoo. Several of the bigger guys start to whisper. Then one of them says, "Hey, kid, what happened to you? You been in a fight with a weed-wacker?"

Everybody laughs. Moss growls.

Mr. Logan stands in front of the class and blows his whistle. I stare at his chunky, unfit frame. His legs are more like tree trunks than legs and are covered in coarse, dark hair. Not to mention, his gut is so big he looks like he could give birth to a 3rd grader.

"Today, we're going to be climbing ropes," he says. He smiles like he enjoys handing out torture. Rope climbing isn't even allowed in schools anymore because of fear of lawsuits, humiliation and broken bones. But Mr. Logan is old-school and never took down the ropes. We could probably report him and get him in big trouble. But nobody wants to cross Logan.

I've never been able to climb those ropes. I'm lucky if I can jump up ten inches and hang on for dear life. Never mind climbing the ten or twelve feet to get to the top. While I dread the next 50 minutes with every ounce of my being, Moss licks his lips, like those ropes are a piece of cake that he can't wait to take a bite out of.

Before Mr. Logan has a chance to blow his whistle again, Moss jumps on a rope and begins climbing toward the rafters of the gym. At first the guys stand there, like they can't decide if he's a show off or just nuts. A couple of the bigger guys look impressed and a little jealous. But then after a few seconds they start to cheer him on. "Go, Tarzan!" somebody yells. Moss is getting the job done in record time.

Once he's at the top he smiles down and pounds his chest with his free hand like he's King Kong and has climbed the Empire State Building. The guys are clapping. I start to applaud, too. It's hard to be jealous of someone who does something so well. He can't read or write, but Moss is a natural athlete.

"That's how it's done, boys." Mr. Logan smiles at Moss like he's found a winning quarterback for our losing football team. "Your turn, Quentin," Mr. Logan adds. "Go up and join your friend."

Moss is at the top of the rope, grinning from ear to ear.

"I think I'll skip rope-climbing today," I say, as if I have a choice.

"I think you misunderstood me, Mr. Moss," he says, sounding like a drill sergeant in the military. "Go attack that rope!"

I amble over with the enthusiasm of a slug and stand on a double mat underneath the rope. Somehow I'm supposed to grab onto the knot, get my feet up to where my head is, and then pull myself forward with pure upper body strength. If I pull this off, it will be the first time in Quentin Moss-physical-education-history.

I take a deep breath and run and leap at the rope. My feet dangle about a foot off the floor as I cling to my nemesis. The rope swings in large, wobbly arcs. Guys laugh. Then somebody starts to make clucking noises like a chicken. Several other guys join in. Meanwhile, Moss hovers above me like a primeval guardian angel, ready to bless me if I'm willing to accept my mission. I hold on as long as I can then fall backward onto the mat with a dull thud. Moss grunts with empathy.

The pain in my butt is the only thing bigger than the laughter from the class.

"Try again, Mr. Moss," Mr. Logan bellows above the laughter.

I drag myself up to face the rope again. I pray for a fire drill or the delivery of an envelope full of Anthrax to rescue me. Then one of the guys points to the ceiling and says, "Hey, look at that."

When I turn around everybody is looking up. Even Mr. Logan has his eyes transfixed on the ceiling. I follow their gaze to see Moss in the rafters, swinging from bar to bar, like he's a trapeze artist in a circus. Except this is no high wire with a net, but a ceiling about 30 feet high, without any mats underneath him. Nobody in the room can believe it. Mr. Logan is so shocked he's not saying anything, and his furry tree legs are shaking like there's an earthquake.

The attention has switched off me and onto Moss. It looks like getting him out of the rafters may take the rest of the class. And I'm pretty sure Moss did it to help me out. It's like we understand each other. As a cave boy he probably knows how important it is to distract a herd of charging rhinos. I see him looking at me and wave. He nods back. Now I owe him.

Food Fight

As soon as gym is over we go to the cafeteria for lunch. Moss is salivating as we stand in line and drool is dripping on his shirt.

"You hungry Moss?" I ask.

"Hungry," Moss repeats, as one of the cafeteria ladies gasps.

"He's harmless," I say, but she doesn't seem to believe me. I wish now that I'd thought to put a hairnet on Moss. Otherwise lunch could get too gross even for me.

The menu today is a pizza slice, midget corn on the cob, and peaches in a cup. Who comes up with these combinations? Not once have I been to a restaurant where pizza is served with corn and peaches. I don't think this is something normal people eat. I can't imagine that the President of the United States is served pizza, corn, and peaches in a cup right there in the Oval Office, along with two cartons of chocolate milk. He might get fed up and start a war.

I survey the crust on the pizza as Moss gobbles it down like it's the best food he's ever tasted. What's more alarming than his appetite is how messy he is. Sure enough, he's eating his own hair with every bite. Bits of crust and corn cob kernels scatter in his wake. He finishes his pizza in three bites, licks the plate clean, and slurps the peaches down in one swallow.

Everybody at the table laughs, like he's doing it to be funny. Why else would anyone eat cafeteria food in thirty seconds flat?

"Hey Quentin, who's the freak?" Jake Hudson yells from the next table. Jake and I used to be friends until he got popular. Now he doesn't want to breathe the same air I breathe.

"He's my cousin," I say to Jake.

"Yeah? Well he acts like he just came out of his cave."

"If you only knew," I say under my breath.

"Does he talk?"

"Not a whole lot," I reply.

"That's weird," Jake says.

"Weird," Moss agrees. He smiles to reveal pieces of corn and peaches sticking between his teeth.

Dex enters the cafeteria and gets his tray, then joins us. "How's it going?" he whispers. "Is anybody onto him?"

"Not yet," I say. I look over at Moss, who's now eating everything on my plate, too. Two teachers look over at him but don't say anything. On Fridays, they let more slide. They're just trying to get through the day like the rest of us.

"At least we don't have to bring him to school tomorrow," I say to Dex.

"What are you going to do with him?" he asks.

I don't think either of us can imagine keeping this secret full time. "I guess I'll try to hide him at my house without my mom finding out. At least until we get him home."

"But what if he's here to stay?" Dex asks.

"I can't think of that right now," I say truthfully.

Moss slurps down what's left of everybody's peach cups at the table. "Do you think he's hungry?" Dex jokes.

"Like a bear," I laugh.

When Moss hears the word, bear, he crouches, on the alert.

"Just kidding," I say to Moss.

He looks at me. I should know better than to joke about bears.

Dex starts on his lunch and has to slap Moss' hand away so he won't eat it. Kids from all over the cafeteria are throwing him their fruit cups and unopened milk cartons and he catches them like he plays for the Atlanta Braves baseball team.

"I wish he would talk to us more," Dex says. "You know, about what his life is like."

"I do, too," I say. "I guess he doesn't have the words. But I think he understands what we're saying. Isn't that right, Moss?" I ask, loud enough for him to hear.

"Right," he says back to me, crushing six empty milk cartons under his fist. Milk sprays all over.

Dex and I watch in disbelief as Moss sticks two straws up his nose like he's pretending to be a walrus. Everybody at the table laughs again, especially Dex, who can relate to having a nose that attracts foreign objects. When he was four he got a lima bean stuck up his nose. His parents didn't realize what had happened until they noticed a strange smell coming from Dex's face. When they took him to the doctor he had to use forceps to pull the bean out of his nostril. The weird part was it had been in there so long it had begun to sprout!

Jake Hudson acts like he doesn't like all the attention Moss is getting. He throws his pizza crust at Moss and it hits him in the shoulder. Moss looks at Jake and snarls.

"He's a regular garbage disposal," Jake says to his friends at the table. They laugh and point at Moss who has Jake's pizza crust sticking out of his mouth.

I look at Dex like 'What should we do now?' Before Dex has time to say anything Jake throws his milk carton with his napkin and straw stuck in the top at Moss. "Let's see if he'll eat garbage, too," he laughs.

Moss catches the milk carton in one hand and throws it back at Jake and hits him right between the eyes and leaves a red mark. A couple of Jake's friends laugh, so Jake reaches over and grabs Moss, but Moss pins his arm to the table until Jake begs him to stop. Moss lets go and Jake storms out of the cafeteria.

As a reward for standing up to Jake, a feat I haven't had the nerve to do, I buy Moss an ice cream. Moss grunts his approval of the ice cream, so I let him eat the wrapper as well.

Seconds later Mr. Richie enters the cafeteria and looks in our direction. Dorky Jake is right behind him. Mr. Richie is as close as our school gets to having a Gestapo. He even has a flat top haircut like a small runway where toy planes could land.

I gasp. Dex sits up straight. Moss has his back to Mr. Richie. He also has chocolate ice cream smeared around his lips that he's licking off with his tongue. He has a really long tongue.

"What do we do?" I whisper to Dex.

"Act normal," Dex whispers back.

I'm wondering how exactly to act normal, since the most abnormal event in my life is happening right now.

"Mr. Moss. Mr. Greenfield," Mr. Richie says to me and Dex. "Mr. Hudson says we've had a little trouble."

Mr. Richie has an obnoxious habit of always calling students by their last names. Meanwhile, Jake lowers his head, stares a hole through his Nikes and rubs his arm where Moss held it.

"Who is your friend?" Mr. Richie leans in to get a closer look at Moss. There's a deep crease on his forehead that makes him look either mean or crazy. Moss lets out one brief honking laugh before he sees my alarm and stops.

"This is Moss," I say. A lump forms in my throat that runs the risk of becoming projectile vomit. Moss and Mr. Richie stare at each other like ancient enemies.

"I see he has a visitor's pass," Mr. Richie says. "But even visitors will be asked to leave if they don't follow the rules."

Moss starts to scratch his head. He eats something that he finds in the tangles.

Mr. Richie grimaces, like Moss is a walking health code violation. "Where exactly are you from?" Mr. Richie asks Moss.

"California!" I chime in.

"Please let Mr. Moss answer," Mr. Richie says.

Moss looks at me like: *What do I do now?*

I look back at him like: *I have no frickin' idea.*

"He has laryngitis," Dex says. "He's lost his voice."

"Laryngitis?" Mr. Richie asks. He eyes Moss. "I want you and your friend, Moss, in the library for seventh period," he says.

Seventh period is two hours from now but I wish it was never. Mr. Richie sends all the kids he considers troublemakers to study hall seventh period. This is the first time I've ever had to go.

Mr. Richie straightens his shoulders and walks out of the cafeteria, Jake at his heels.

"We got study hall, but at least he didn't throw me or Moss out of school," I say.

"Study hall sucks though," Dex says.

"Sucks," Moss agrees, even though he has no idea what a 'study hall' is.

"I'm glad Moss stood up to Jake," I say. "But that was too close."

"Too close," Dex agrees.

"Too close," Moss echoes.

Ancestors

When we go into my history class Mrs. Henry is setting up a laptop and projector the library sent over. Of all my teachers she would be the one to turn Moss in if he starts grunting or something. She always plays by the rules. This is a shame, because I love history otherwise. History was never played by the rules.

"Today we're starting a new unit on prehistoric cave man," she says as we take our seats.

No way! Is this a weird coincidence or what? I raise my eyebrows and look over at Moss, our very own example sitting right next to me.

"Prehistoric means pre-history, before humans began documenting things," she continues. "Which means archaeologists and historians have had to piece together evidence to determine what life was like back then."

I wonder what Mrs. Henry would do if she knew there was a witness to pre-history sitting on the back row of her classroom.

Moss scratches his head and looks at the illustrated timeline on the wall like he's trying to connect the dots between this world and his.

My dad's family did a family tree that shows how our ancestors came over from England in the early 1800s. It shows six generations of the Moss family. If cave boy Moss were to do the same it would be more like 60,000 generations. It's strange to think that Moss' family is one of the first families to ever exist.

I glance over at him with new appreciation. When I look at him I see where Homo sapiens evolved from. And when he looks at me he can see where humankind is going. Between the two of us, it isn't just a family tree but an entire forest.

I pick my nose. The Dalai Lama moment fades.

Mrs. Henry is preoccupied with the laptop, so she doesn't ask who Moss is. Mrs. Henry is near retirement and anything invented in the last twenty years is a challenge for her. When the lights go off and the documentary starts I think we're home free. But when the larger than life images appear on the screen Moss leaps onto a nearby table. Several kids giggle. I jerk Moss down so fast I'm surprised I don't pull his shoulder out of joint. A second too late, Mrs. Henry turns and squints into the dark classroom.

Moss grunts his fascination with the documentary, like it's a big book with pictures. The film shows what scientists think life was like back then. Except that for Moss, *back then* was sometime early this morning. He tugs at my arm, with a look of awe and terror, like a little kid who's meeting Santa Claus for the first time.

"Shhh," I say.

He tugs at my arm again and points at the drawings on the screen.

"Shhh," I say louder, but it doesn't do any good.

Mrs. Henry turns and looks in our direction again, but the room is still too dark to see.

When the photographs of cave drawings come on I have to hold Moss down so he doesn't lurch at the screen. It's like he doesn't have words for what he's feeling so he's whining like Coltrane does when he needs to go outside. More kids laugh, but luckily Mrs. Henry hasn't been able to tell who's making the noise. With every new scene Moss grunts or whines. The laughter from our side of the room gets louder.

"What's going on?" Mrs. Henry asks. She fumbles with the laptop and turns off the documentary. When she walks to our side of the room, I bend over and moan like I'm having the worst stomach ache of my life. The closer she gets the louder I wail. Even Moss looks concerned.

"Quentin, are you all right?" Mrs. Henry asks. The only light is from the hallway which reflects off her glasses and makes her look like she's dressed up for Halloween.

"It must have been something I ate," I say, moaning again. Having Moss around has brought out the actor in me. Instead of trying not to be noticed—a position I decided is the safest in middle school—I'm drawing attention to myself. This is dangerous, but what's more dangerous is Moss being found out and both of us being ushered into Mr. Richie's office where he calls the people who carry clubs, as well as CNN. That kind of attention I could live without my whole life.

"Quentin, do you need to go to the bathroom?" Mrs. Henry asks in a loud whisper. I stifle a laugh.

"No, I'm fine," I say. I'm doubled over but can see Moss sitting quietly in his chair.

"You have my permission to leave if you need to," Mrs. Henry says, as if my bowels may explode at any moment.

With a straight face, I thank her and she walks away. Between the difficulties with the electronic equipment and my outburst, she's forgotten about Moss, and turns on the documentary again.

Toward the end of the video there's real footage of an ancient cave somewhere in Europe. I wonder if it's the same cave Mr. G. was talking about in English. When I look over I see tears in Moss' eyes and I almost tear up, too. His grunts change to moans mixed with a whimper or two. A couple of girls turn to look at him. Their eyes soften like they feel sorry for him and would go on a date with him if he asked.

In that moment, I feel responsible for dreaming him up, and I wish I knew how to get him back so he can see his family again and visit his cave friends. I know what it's like to feel like you don't have any of your clan around. Especially since Dad left. He was the only one in our family who understood me. I try to imagine hundreds of years from now somebody showing a documentary of what my life was like. I would be sad, too. Who knows? I might even long to hear *The Voice* and see *The Look,* though it's hard to imagine missing my sister, Katie.

The video ends and everybody groans when the lights go on again. Several people look like they're just waking up from a good nap.

"What do you think it was like to live in prehistoric times?" Mrs. Henry asks the class. On most days I avoid eye contact or she might call on me, but this time I look straight at her. I even raise my hand.

When she sees my hand go up she looks as surprised as I am. "Yes, Quentin?"

"I think it was a hard life, but also exciting and cool," I say.

"Cool?" she asks.

"Yeah," I say. "For one thing, you wouldn't ever have to take a bath. For another thing, you wouldn't have to go to school."

People laugh.

"I can see how those things might appeal to someone your age," she says. "If Quentin is right, what do you think were the hard things?" she asks the class.

I wish Moss could answer. When nobody else raises their hand I raise mine again.

"Yes, Quentin?" Mrs. Henry asks, as if lightning has struck the same place twice.

"I think you'd have to grow up really fast. And you'd have to work really hard, because nothing like we have today was invented yet. And you'd have to learn to be brave, I think.

You'd have to do things on your own a lot. Maybe you wouldn't even have a dad."

Mrs. Henry pauses. "Well done, Quentin," she says, looking kind of proud of me. My classmates are over the novelty of me speaking up and are now glaring over at me like I'm making them look bad.

A knock on the door interrupts our discussion. The principal, Mr. Proctor, a.k.a. *Big Voice*, comes in. I'm glad it's not Mr. Richie, but my palms get sweaty anyway because I'm wondering if Mr. Richie gave him the heads up about Moss.

To my relief, Mr. Proctor is there on other business. *Big Voice* introduces a new girl to the class who makes Heather Parker look like a scrawny mutt from the animal shelter. Moss watches me watch her. Then he grunts, smiles, and nudges me in the ribs with his elbow in a universal guy language which almost knocks me off my chair.

My face flushes red. But nobody else notices because they're all sizing up the new girl.

"Fire," Moss says, pointing to my blushing face.

"Don't start," I whisper to him.

Truth is, I'm a coward when it comes to girls. You'd think I'd have all sorts of experience with females since I live with two of them, but it doesn't help. I'm still living in the Stone Age when it comes to getting girls to notice me. Moss seems to know that about me without me even saying a word. He puts a brotherly arm around me like he promises to teach me everything he knows. Family comes in all shapes, sizes and time periods.

Elvis Has Left the Building

After the bell rings we make our way to my next class: band. The new girl's name is Alicia and she's in band, too. She plays French horn and if I look over the top of my music stand, past the flutes and clarinets, I can see her eyes. She doesn't look up much from the music, probably because she doesn't know anybody yet.

I play my dad's old saxophone that he used to play when he was my age. A rubber band holds one of the key pads together and the tarnish looks like a bad case of metallic chicken pox, but it still works.

Right behind Alicia, Moss stands in the percussion section. The guys back there are close to being primitive themselves. They're showing Moss how to beat the bass drum. Moss is good, and I wonder if he's beat on drums before. Maybe that's how cave teenagers sent messages before you could text.

For the longest time I watch Alicia. I fantasize about her looking across the band room and falling under the spell of my good looks. While we're playing our warm-up scales, I pretend to be all serious, in order to win Alicia over with my passion for playing the saxophone. Then our band director, Mr. Davis, who looks like the human version of Homer Simpson, cuts off the band, except I don't see him, so I keep playing after everybody else has stopped. My squawking saxophone cries out like the mating call of the biggest goose of all time.

Mr. Davis tilts his Homer Simpson head and says, *huh?* Then he looks at me and says, "Mr. Moss, may I ask what planet you're on?"

The whole band explodes in laughter, because Mr. Davis has a funny way of humiliating a person. Meanwhile, I fall back to planet earth in crashing speed, still trying to determine the exact color of Alicia's eyes.

I slump in my seat and don't have the courage to look in Alicia's direction because my face is flushing so hot I figure the tips of my ears must be turning red, too. In my imagination I hear Heather Parker's mocking voice: *Forget the gums, look at his ears!* At that moment I want to crawl under the biggest rock in Atlanta and hang out with the worms. Just when I thought nothing could be more humiliating than Heather Parker's rejection or the rope-climbing incident, this is even worse!

In the next second Moss starts playing a solo on the drums. Everybody turns to watch. The guys step back as he takes over the entire drum section. Moss beats the timpani drums, then the bongos, and then plays the snare drums, creating this amazing jungle rhythm that has everybody tapping their feet. At first Mr. Davis tries to stop him, but then he starts clapping along.

Moss has everybody captivated by his primitive beat. Everybody is beating on their music stands with their hands and stomping their feet. It's like we're all remembering our jungle roots, a time when life had a rhythm to it and wasn't so complicated. Moss keeps playing, using so many different sounds and beats that the entire trombone section is dancing to it and dipping their trombones up and down. Then the tuba section joins in and then the flutes.

After he plays a flurry of drum rolls, he points a drum stick in my direction like it's my turn for a solo. He keeps the beat going, and keeps motioning for me to join in. I pick up my saxophone and improvise to the beat like the jazz solos Dex and I have listened to on different recordings. Even though we didn't get to hear that special band in Underground Atlanta, all that listening to my dad's records pays off.

Moss' beat is inspiring me because I'm playing saxophone jazz riffs better than I've ever played in my life. We go on for several minutes, everybody clapping to the beat, and then we build up to a finale.

Silence follows. This could very well be my most humiliating moment ever, which means I'll have to get a passport and move to Iceland or Finland or one of those other cold places. But then everybody applauds.

Mr. Davis yells, "Bravo, bravo!" like they do at symphony concerts. It's the loudest standing ovation I've ever heard. I join Moss in the percussion section, and we bow together like we're at Carnegie Hall and we've given the performance of our lives. Before I know it, my humiliating moment morphs into a surprising victory. Everybody continues to clap and whistle. We take another bow. I notice Alicia smiling at us. I've never been the star of anything before, but this feels great.

Moss has a huge grin on his face. Music is the universal language. I think Moss knew that even before I did. For someone from another age he sure is smart. Primitive doesn't mean you're stupid, I guess. It just means you're from an earlier, simpler time.

Moss and I take a final bow and saunter out the side door of the band room like rock stars leaving a stage. *Quentin Moss has left the building.*

Hiccups

I'm still smiling from band but my smile fades when we get to the last period of the day, study hall. Mr. Richie is nowhere in sight. A couple of guys are tossing a football in the back corners of the library so I pull Moss in the opposite direction. We walk past the big aquarium and Moss stops to watch the exotic fish swim around. I don't know what's going through his mind, but I have a feeling after all that drumming he's considering sushi. Mrs. Gilbert, the librarian, wouldn't go for that at all. She talks to those fish like they're her relatives.

We take a corner table and I grab a library book from the back shelf on famous paintings in the world and plop it down in front of Moss. Nothing distracts my prehistoric visitor more than a bunch of pictures. "This is art," I whisper, pointing to the first picture.

"Art?" he asks.

"Drawings, like in caves."

"Art," he nods.

It's like Moss and I are becoming buddies. And I like how he has a way of turning things around when they aren't going my way. But what's got me baffled is how he's still here. Any dream I've ever had in the past faded fast. Moss hasn't faded in the least. If anything he's getting more real.

Moss is like a genie that I can't figure out how to get back into the bottle. I look over and smile at him. He's making the best of it, that's for sure. But I can tell he wants to get back home. I wrack my brain for a solution and decide I need somebody much smarter than me to find an answer. I need Dad.

My frustration builds. Even when I call his cell phone he doesn't always answer. It's like someone in Oregon dreamed him up and he hasn't been able to get home, either. If I were smart I'd figure out how to make Moss disappear and make my dad reappear.

"You were great playing those drums," I whisper to Moss.

"Great," he smiles. "Girl go--" he claps, like he noticed Alicia, too.

"Yeah, she did clap," I say, feeling pleased.

While Moss looks at pictures, I remember the details of my dream. In my memory I see where Moss lives, his dark cave, and a fire burning inside. His bed is a pile of straw and animal hides and there are animal bones lying around. Furs, antlers, skulls. I zone in on the dream, remembering things I didn't notice before, like the drawings on the far wall. There are animals painted on them, as well as spears and arrows, similar to what was in the documentary Mrs. Henry showed us in history.

"Did you draw art in your cave?" I ask.

"Draw art," Moss repeats. He doesn't look up from the book.

"That's probably why you like all those pictures," I say. "You're an artist."

"Artist?" he asks. He looks over at me.

"I bet you'll be a famous artist," I say. "I bet someday they'll show pictures of your art in history classes."

Moss shrugs like fame doesn't interest him.

I'm not sure I'd like to live in Moss' world. Who wants to work that hard? Even getting a drink of water requires finding a stream or waterfall, when all we have to do is turn on a faucet. Some things never change, though. My memory flashes on Moss' mom yelling for him to get up. I guess every kid wants to sleep in. Moss might be tired of his mom's voice, too. And there wasn't a father around in the dream. But maybe his dad was out on a hunting party. Or maybe he isn't part of the picture anymore, like mine.

It's strange to think that even though his world is thousands of years older, Moss and I have similar lives, with friends, family, and dreams. In other ways our lives are different. Sure, he has a lot of freedom where he's from, but it must be dangerous all the time, too. Even to get a drink from a stream you'd always have to be looking over your shoulder to make sure some giant prehistoric predator hasn't chosen you for its meal.

Mr. Richie walks in and the boys throwing the football stop. Mr. Richie eyes me and Moss like we're convicts on death row. I've never been in any real trouble a day in my life, but Mr. Richie treats me like I'm a multiple felon.

Moss begins a low growl behind his teeth. I kick his leg under the table and he stops. Moss could take out Mr. Richie in a fight. But Mr. Richie is the least of my worries now. I've got to get Moss back to his cave.

Dex enters the library and walks toward our table. "What are you doing here?" I whisper. "Did you get in trouble?"

"Nah, I just asked Miss Snyder if I could do research for my term paper." Dex and Moss greet each other with fist bumps. Dex can get along with anybody. It doesn't matter which eon they're from.

Moss shows Dex a painting by Picasso from the art book. Moss crosses his eyes like he's trying to imitate the eyes in the painting. Dex smiles. Mr. Richie glares over from where he's perched near the door like a prison guard. He points to his eye, then points at me to tell me that he has his *eye* on me. I look down at the book. As long as he has his eye on me and not Moss I'm fine with that. It's trying to explain Moss that threatens to put an end to my middle school career. Hmm. I consider confessing Moss' true identity.

"You have to help me figure out what to do with Moss," I whisper to Dex.

"You mean right now?" Dex whispers back. "He seems to be pretty happy."

"No, how to get him back home," I say.

"Maybe there's a flight on Frontier Airlines," Dex says.

"Think of the frequent flyer miles he would get. My dad has a zillion, and he only flies to New York."

"Ha, ha," I whisper to Dex. "I'm serious. What am I going to do with him? What if I can't get him back?"

"Do you think your mom would like another son?" Dex asks, a dumb grin on his face.

"I'm not sure she wants the one she has," I say.

Dex looks at me like we both know that's not true. Not really. We think for a while. "Maybe we should ask your dad what to do," Dex whispers. "He was always good at stuff like this. Remember when he took us to that museum in Washington, D.C. He had all the metro stops figured out."

"This is a little more complicated than metro stops," I say.

Dex nods his agreement. But I remember that trip to the Smithsonian Natural History Museum. We were seven. That's when I first started getting interested in history. For every birthday and Christmas after that, one of my gifts has been a book on some part of history. But all of those books combined couldn't prepare me for having history materialize right in front of me.

"We need one of those transporter things they had in those old Star Trek movies," Dex whispers.

I think about how he got here in the first place. The transporter was my dream. "Hey, maybe I can dream him back," I say to Dex. In my excitement I use my regular voice. Both Mrs. Gilbert and Mr. Richie shoot their gaze in my direction. My face turns hot and undoubtedly red. Mr. Richie walks toward us, but then he stops when the office calls him over his cell phone. He leaves. I exhale. Moss exhales. Everybody in the room exhales their relief.

"Dream him back?" Dex says thoughtfully. "You know, it might work. Like you said, it's how he got here in the first place." Dex thinks some more. "Are you sleepy now?" he asks, like maybe a nap would do the trick.

I look at him like he's just suggested I strip down to my boxer shorts in front of everybody in the library and strap on my retainer headgear. "Not even a little," I say. "But I guess I can try it tonight. That is, unless somebody catches on and we end up in FBI custody or on Inside Edition."

"It's worth a try," Dex says.

I have no idea how to pull this off. I don't understand how dreams work in forward motion, much less in reverse. The final bell rings and Moss, Dex and I fight our way through the crowded hallway to the lockers and then outside.

As the crowd clears we see the new girl, Alicia, waiting for her ride. Dex and Moss nudge me toward her. I resist. But when I'm not expecting it Dex and Moss team up and give me a good push. I yelp as I fall at Alicia's feet.

"Sorry," I say. It is the first of a long string of apologies I offer. In fact, I can't seem to stop apologizing. Dex and Moss look over at me like I not only have a disgusting case of diarrhea of the mouth, but also a bad case of low self-esteem.

Alicia huffs her irritation. She turns away so fast the wind from her hair hits me in the face. But her hair smells good and makes me smile. Dex and Moss continue to look at me like

I've sprouted four heads and none of them work well. They motion for me to try again. At that moment I'm wishing someone would have a dream and transport me to a deserted planet where I can live out the rest of my life alone. Against my better judgment, I approach Alicia again.

"Uh, hi Alicia," I say timidly. "I'm Quentin Moss."

She glances at me, then over at Dex and Moss. She does a double take on Moss before looking away, a common reaction to seeing him up close.

Dex gives me another jab, this time with his elbow. It hurts. "How was your first day?" I ask Alicia, wincing from Dex's encouragement.

"It was okay," she says. Her eyes stay focused on the school's driveway.

"That's good," I say. I'm already running out of things to say. Any confidence I had left drains out of my body with the sweat that I'm producing in buckets. I begin to hiccup. Dex's eyes widen. He knows what this means. When I get really nervous I get hiccups. Not quiet, barely noticeable blips that girls think are cute. But loud, body-jerking spasms that the general population fears might be contagious. In a matter of seconds I have the *worst* hiccups I've ever had in my life. Dex and Moss watch in compassionate horror as my whole body convulses every five to ten seconds in a sharp, distinctive *hic-cup*. I sound like a giant, hic-cupping, toad.

My face changes from red to the color of an overzealous beet. I hold my breath and count to ten. Nothing helps. Sweat pools in my sneakers as Alicia watches every convulsion.

Right when I'm trying to figure out how to get Moss back to the Stone Age and take me with him, Alicia says, "You're funny, Quentin," as if the show is for her benefit.

I smile between spasms.

"Hey, aren't you the friend of the drummer?" she adds.

"Yeah, that was Moss." I gesture in Moss' direction.

She smiles over at Moss. I don't like the shift in her attention.

"I was the one playing the saxophone," I say. I give her my best smile—minus the gums—before hiccupping again.

Moss ambles over and slaps me on the back, like he's proud of me for not barfing or running away. He gives a jovial grunt.

"Did he grunt?" Alicia asks.

"Oh, uh, yeah," I say. "Well, there's a reason for that." I pause in brief horror as I try to think up the reason. "Uh, he hasn't talked much since the accident."

"The accident?" she asks, a curious look on her face.

"The accident?" Dex repeats, his curiosity peaked, as well.

"Yeah, the accident," I say. I glance over at Dex and scream help with my eyes.

"Oh, yeah, the accident," Dex says. He catches on to what I'm doing. "Horrible accident," he adds. "One of the worst accidents ever."

Alicia looks at Moss again, who is eying the zipper on an 8th graders backpack. "But he seemed okay when he was playing the drums."

"Yeah, it comes and goes. Mostly, he's okay," I reassure her between hiccups. "But he doesn't talk much. *Hasn't since the accident,*" I whisper.

"Oh," she says with sadness. She looks again in Moss' direction. "Well, I hope he gets better soon."

"I'm sure he will," I say. "But don't be surprised if he grunts or anything. He hasn't gotten all of his speech back yet."

"Oh," she says again, giving Moss a compassionate smile.

Moss smiles back, like his dream is getting better with every flutter of her eye lashes. I pull him away from the backpack and punch him in the ribs so he'll remember whose territory he's in. Seconds later Alicia's mom arrives and she has to leave. Before she closes the door Moss grabs the car door and acts like he's going to get in the car with Alicia. Dex and I grab Moss and pull him back to the curb. As they're driving away, I realize my hiccups are gone. Maybe they got scared out of me because for a second it looked like Moss was going to get the girl instead of me.

If I added up all the humiliating moments in my life there are probably hundreds of them. The latest being: I try to impress a girl and end up with the worst case of hiccups in adolescent history. But then there was the time Katie accidentally dyed my hair orange when she convinced me that blond high-lights would attract girls. (Two cautions: Never listen to a sister that hates you most of the time and always read the directions.) And there was the time after it rained that I tripped and did a swan dive in the hallway in front of the school office. (Mats are at the front door for a reason.) And the time after Dad told me about Heather, that I got so angry that I accidentally told him that I never wanted to see him again. (I think he took me up on it.)

But all in all, thanks to Moss bailing me out a couple of times, what could have been a disastrous day at school turned out okay, in fact better than okay.

Action Hero

Moss, Dex and I ride the school bus home and get off a stop early to go to the convenience store for snacks. Dex picks up a big bag of chips and three Cokes while Moss opens and closes every single one of the refrigerated section doors at least twice. I wander up front and read the sensational headlines in *The National Enquirer:* Wolf Boy Discovered in Louisiana. I imagine the story of Moss splattered on the front page! *Cave Boy Discovered in Atlanta.* I shudder.

A couple of guys in their twenties come in with baseball caps pulled low over their eyes. One of them, who reeks of cigarettes and beer, shoves me out of the way so he can get to the counter.

"Hey, watch what you're doing," I say.

The guy stiff arms me again, pushing me further away. I join Dex and Moss at the back of the store. The cashier, an older Asian man, looks nervous. He keeps glancing in our direction. The second guy canvases the place. He looks down every aisle of the small store. I don't know what he's looking for. When he sees Moss and Dex by the canned sodas he hesitates for a second, and then grins. Come to think of it they do make a funny looking pair.

The guy up front asks the cashier for a pack of cigarettes. He keeps tugging up his pants every few seconds, like Moss played with his zipper at first. The second guy joins him at the front. He has his hand in his jacket pocket.

All of a sudden the two guys are yelling at the cashier. They tell him to give them the money in the cash drawer. Dex and I look over at each other, not knowing what to do. It's like a scene out of a movie. If we run away we have to go right by the bad guys. My heart races to catch up with my thoughts and my body shakes. I've never been so scared in my life and Dex looks just as scared as I am. If I didn't know it was his natural look, I'd think his hair was standing on end from fright.

Moss grunts and runs toward the two guys, like he's turned into a cave boy action hero. He makes a flying leap at the two guys and tackles them to the floor. They cuss at Moss and get up. Then they come after him. Moss butts one of the guys in the stomach with his head. The guy falls to the floor moaning like crazy. Then Moss growls at the second guy who stops and rethinks his next move. Instead of coming after Moss he runs out the door like a charging mastodon is after him. Moss smiles.

Dex and I stand frozen in disbelief. We hear sirens in the distance. The guy he butted in the stomach is still on the floor moaning, curled up in a ball. When he hears the sirens he gets up and runs away, too.

"We've got to get out of here," I say to Dex. "How will we explain Moss?"

Dex gives the shaken cashier a five dollar bill for our chips and sodas and doesn't wait for the change.

"Wait a minute," the cashier says. "Your friend here is a hero."

"He's not a hero. He's just a regular kid," I say. I glance over at Moss who doesn't look like a regular kid at all. "Sorry, but we've got to go," I add. I grab Moss' shirt and pull him out the door. The sirens get louder. We take the side street to our neighborhood. We're running like we're the crooks because we don't know what else to do. We don't slow down until we reach the next street.

Dex and I are breathing heavy, but Moss isn't the least bit winded. Dex and I lean over to catch our breath. I have to admit I'm impressed. Moss didn't hesitate for a second. He took on both those guys and didn't get a scratch. Maybe he is a hero.

We walk in the direction of our neighborhood. Three blocks later we arrive at Dex's house. We didn't do anything wrong but we're nervous that the police will want to ask us questions. We duck through the shrubs into Dex's backyard where we won't be found.

Nobody's ever home at Dex's house. Most of the time not even Dex, since he spends so much time with me. We take the sodas and chips and sit on the top of an old picnic table.

"That was unbelievable," I say. My shaking finally stops.

Dex nods. He still looks like he's in shock. Or maybe that's just his hair.

"Did you see Moss take those guys out?" I say. He did everything I wish I had the guts to do.

"Two at once. Just like that. Piece of cake," Dex says.

We look at Moss in admiration. He shrugs like he doesn't get what the big deal is.

"Head butt to the gut," Dex says. "Very effective." He punches Moss in the arm, but Moss doesn't even flinch.

But everybody has things they're afraid of. When we pop open the sodas, the spewing Coke scares Moss so bad he jumps backward in a reverse long-jump that any track star would envy.

I reassure Moss that carbonation is nothing to be frightened of, but he doesn't believe me. When I try to get him to drink, Moss grunts, like he's not so sure he wants to.

"Like this," Dex says to Moss. He takes several big gulps.

Moss imitates him and starts sneezing like a dozen fossilized gnats have flown up his nose. I guess carbonated sodas seem a little different if you've been drinking from streams your whole life.

Moss keeps rubbing his nose as Dex and I each grab a handful of potato chips. Before we've had time to finish what's in our hands, Moss has devoured the rest of the bag and is licking the salt off his fingers that he hasn't washed all day. By now he's thirsty and sips the soda with a big grin on his face. I feel a little guilty for introducing him to junk food, because whatever he was eating before has made him stronger than Dex and I put together.

Moss sees an azalea bush and goes over and gives it a good watering, like he's been waiting all day to find a decent bathroom. Dex and I don't have the heart to stop him. Nobody can see into Dex's backyard anyway. In a moment of guy-bonding, we join him. Moss smiles and grunts like he's found his clan.

"Weren't you scared?" I ask Moss after we finish.

"Scared?" he repeats.

"Yeah, weren't you afraid those guys would cream you?"

Moss tilts his head like Coltrane does sometimes when he's trying to understand.

"I was plenty scared," Dex says.

"Me, too," I say. "Do you think those creeps had guns?"

"I think the short one did," Dex says.

"Well, we had a secret weapon ourselves," I smile. "Moss, the amazing cave boy."

"He was awesome," Dex says. "He was probably operating on pure adrenaline. You know, like when moms lift cars off their kids."

Moss finishes his soda and is now eating Dex's potato chips. He crams a fistful in his mouth.

"If Moss ends up staying, I don't know how I'm going to feed him," I say to Dex. "He eats enough for ten kids."

Dex nods.

Before I have time to figure out how I'm going to buy mass quantities of food on my meager allowance, Moss holds his stomach. Then he gets a goofy look on his face like an alien is about to burst out of his skin and lets out a belch to end all belches.

A gaseous fog of Coke and potato chips fans out in our direction. Dex and I cover our noses, and then start laughing. We laugh until our stomachs hurt. Moss laughs, too, and it sounds like an entire flock of Canada geese are coming in for a landing in Dex's backyard. The laughing feels good after being so scared before.

Not one to be outdone, I put a hand under my armpit and start pumping like I'm playing an accordion, unleashing a chorus of arm farts. The three of us roll around on the ground, grunting and laughing like this is the funniest thing ever. We're like three primitive cave boys bonding during an ancient initiation rite. Except instead of having to survive in the wilderness, we have to survive armed robbers and belching arm-farts.

"Quentin, funny," Moss says. At that moment he looks proud of me.

"Thanks," I say. I jump up on the picnic table and take a bow for my arm-farting concert, which was almost as good as my saxophone solo earlier. But Moss is the real star of the day.

Road Trip

Since Dex's parents won't be home until late, Dex's back-yard is a perfect hiding place for Moss. I can't imagine the police going door to door to search for witnesses of a foiled crime, but it makes sense to lay low anyway.

"Hey, we already have a getaway car if we need it," Dex says. He points to the faded blue Honda in the back driveway that's on its way to becoming extinct. His dad drove the Civic in college, and he's been saving it for Dex until he gets old enough to drive. We have spent endless hours daydreaming about where this car will take us some day. As far as I know my dad hasn't saved me anything. He did leave an old license plate in the garage from when he lived in Minnesota after college, and a snow shovel that we've never used in Georgia, not even once.

We show Moss the Honda. We work on it almost every day after school. Or at least we pretend to work on it. Most of the time we just take out a part, shake it a few times, blow on it and then clean it off before putting it right back in again.

Dex opens the creaky hood. The three of us peer inside at the gray, dusty engine, like there's a magic carpet inside if we can figure out how to make it work. Come to think of it, a magic carpet might come in handy for getting Moss back home.

It's weird to see Moss admiring something that won't even be invented for thousands of years. He pulls a couple of hoses and twists the oil cap a few times, then wipes grease on his face. He looks like the original prehistoric Honda mechanic. Then we notice that one of the hoses under the hood is moving. We look closer and see that it's a big rat snake about as thick as one of my wrists that's made his home under the hood. Dex and I scream a primordial scream and jump back.

Moss looks at us like *what's the big deal?* And grabs the snake and flings it against a nearby oak tree. Dex and I gasp in glorified horror. Did he really do that? The snake lies limp and dead at the base of the tree. Moss smiles, then pats us both on the back and walks over to the snake. He picks it up, takes a good look at it and even licks his lips before he flings it into the bushes. Would this be food for him? I guess we're lucky that he's already full of chips and soda. For the first time we get a glimpse of what Moss' life must be like.

"Good job, man," Dex says. "First you take out two criminals and now a snake."

Moss nods.

I thank Moss, too, and at the same time realize what a wimp I am. I wouldn't have grabbed that snake in a million years. Nor would I have taken on those two criminals.

Still in shock, we get inside the Civic. Dex gets in the driver's seat, I'm in the passenger side and Moss gets in the back seat.

"This would be a good get-away car," Dex says, his hands on the steering wheel.

I'm thinking this would be like the worst get-away car in history. It barely even runs, but I don't tell Dex that.

"Where do you guys want to go?" Dex asks me and Moss.

"Go?" Moss asks.

"Yeah, where do you want to go?"

"Home," he says.

Dex and I look at each other. Neither of us knows how to give Moss what he wants, given this old Honda isn't a time machine.

I have to admire how calm Moss is, even if he is a little homesick. I'd be panicking right now if I were in his shoes, though Moss doesn't actually have shoes, since he borrowed a pair of mine.

"Well, maybe we could go to China," I say, changing the subject so Moss won't feel bad.

Moss grunts like it's an interesting possibility, but I'm pretty sure he has no idea what China is—the country or the dishes.

"It's hard to get to China in a car," Dex says. He looks out through the windshield toward our future.

We sit in silence, thinking up possibilities. "How about Alaska?" Dex asks finally. "I hear you can see Russia from there."

"I guess we could drive there," I say, "as long as we don't have to cross any oceans." I wonder if a car with 280,000 miles on it can make it to Alaska.

"I'll MapQuest it later and see how far it is," Dex says. "The police would never find us there."

We both like the idea of far away. We turn and look at Moss. He smiles like he likes the idea.

"We should start saving money for gas," I say.

"Good idea," Dex replies.

I fish into my pocket for spare change and add up one dollar and 53 cents. "This will get us started I guess." I put the money in the glove compartment next to a petrified chocolate bar that melted on top of the owner's manual when Dex's dad was still in college.

"I wonder if it's as cold in Alaska as people say," Dex asks. He digs in his pocket and throws in 75 cents. Moss digs in his pocket and throws in what looks like a mouse skeleton and a piece of flint. I close the glove compartment.

"We'll have to fill the car with antifreeze if we go to Alaska," I say.

"That'll be another couple of bucks," Dex says.

"We'll manage," I say. I look back at Moss who is now rolling the window up and down with impressive speed. "Hey, you want to go to Alaska, Moss?"

"Alaska," Moss says. He studies the handle of the window.

"You're going to have to give up those clothes you're used to wearing," I say. "Furry underwear won't make it."

"He wears furry underwear?" Dex asks. He opens one eye wider than the other.

"Animal skins," I say. "I hid them in my closet."

Dex shudders. "Do you think he had to kill his underwear himself?"

"Probably," I say.

"Cool!" Dex says. He puts the key in the ignition and turns the radio on. The tuner is already set on our favorite station. Moss is turning his head from side to side like he's a satellite picking up signals. It's hard to imagine someone our age hearing a radio for the first time. Dex starts to show off and turns the sound up so loud the bass rattles the change in the glove compartment. Moss covers his ears and howls like a wolf baying at the moon. I make Dex turn the radio down. Moss hasn't jumped into any bushes for a while, and I don't want him to start now. It's funny how brave he was with the thieves and the snake but he's scared to death of technology. Maybe he knows something we don't know.

Just as a special news report comes on, the station fades. I'm wondering if it was something about the robbery.

I give the radio a slap. Dex looks at me like I've just slapped him instead of his clunker car. Since the car is never driven, the battery wears down a lot. More than once we've had to jump-start Dex's car off his dad's, which is always there when his dad is out of town. We keep jumper cables in the trunk and are getting good at recharging that old battery in record breaking speed. Sometimes we pretend to work for the pit crew at the Indy 500.

With the windows rolled up, the car is stuffy and smells like a combination of Armor All, potato chip belches, and a boy's locker room.

"Don't take this personally, Quentin, but you smell," Dex says.

"That's Moss," I say, whose odor has ripened as the day progresses.

"No, Quentin, I think your aftershave has turned sour," Dex says. "When are you going to quit wearing that stuff?"

The smell of Armor All competes with my aftershave.

"Your car doesn't smell so great, either," I say. "The Armor All on the dashboard is an inch thick."

"Well, that aftershave you've got on makes me want to throw up," Dex says.

"Throw up," Moss repeats, as if he could use another snack.

"If we touch the dashboard we leave fingerprints," I say. "Which is fine if we're putting together an FBI crime file."

Dex shrugs like he's become Moss and doesn't have anything to say. Smells are about the only thing Dex and I disagree on.

I look at Moss, who shrugs, too, then belches again.

"Throw up?" he asks.

"No, that's a burp. Throwing up is something else," I say.

Dex laughs. "We have a chance to move history forward, but instead we're teaching our prehistoric ancestor the difference between throwing up and belching."

I laugh, too, while Moss practices burping in the back seat.

"Well, I'm not the only one who smells," I say, returning to our earlier conversation. I nod toward the back seat.

"Yeah, but he has an excuse," Dex says.

"Like what?" I say.

"Like he lives in a cave and hasn't used soap a day of his life."

"Well, I'm not giving up my aftershave until you give up your Armor All," I say to Dex.

"I'm not giving up my Armor All until you give up your aftershave," Dex says back.

"I'm not giving up my aftershave," I counter.

Dex takes a cloth from under his seat and rubs on another think layer of Armor All to the dashboard. The odor in the car overtakes us. Moss makes hacking noises like he's swallowed a bug. Now an expert, he rolls down the window with impressive speed and spits a huge hocker outside.

"We're probably killing billions of brain cells with that junk," I say, grateful for the fresh air.

"So what?" Dex says.

"So, when we're old, we'll probably need adult diapers," I say.

"You watch too much cable TV," Dex replies.

"TV?" Moss says.

"Don't ask," we say in unison.

Before dark, Dex stands guard at my front door as we prepare to sneak Moss back into my house. A police car drives by the front of the house as Moss and I hide in the bushes. Once the cop passes, we push Moss inside and close the front door.

"Do you think they're looking for those thieves?" I ask Dex.

"I don't know," Dex says. "But keep Moss hidden the rest of the night. We don't want anybody questioning him."

"Don't worry," I say.

We can hear my mom making dinner in the kitchen. Moss starts to lick one of the large houseplants in the entryway. "Why does he do stuff like that?" I whisper to Dex.

Dex shrugs.

We lead Moss up the stairs. Dex checks to make sure Katie is nowhere around. Then we pull Moss into my room.

"I still can't believe what happened at the convenience store," I say.

"No kidding," Dex replies.

"Seriously, do you think the cops will come looking for us?" I ask.

"No, we didn't do anything wrong," Dex says. "I guess we could describe the guys. But the cashier could do that, too. I don't think we have anything to worry about."

"Good," I say. "I don't think I can take any more excitement in one day."

This may be the truest thing I've ever said. I never thought so much could happen in one day, and I still haven't figured out how to get Moss home again.

Ancient Rituals

"You're awfully quiet, Quentin," *The Voice* says at dinner. "Tell me about your day."

I clam up a lot with *The Voice*, but it isn't that I don't have anything to say. It's that my words hang out in my head for a while before I'm ready to talk to her. Not that I could even begin to tell her about my day.

"My day was fine," I say. I slip a meatball into my napkin to take to Moss. Coltrane sniffs the napkin from under the table. Moss is in my room and probably starving. I remember my goldfish, Henry the VIII, on the top of my dresser, and wonder if he's already history. There were seven other goldfish named Henry that came before him, over the span of about three years. But I'm not about to tell my mom that I'm concerned that the latest Henry might be eaten by a prehistoric teenager.

"He's hiding something, Mom," my sister says. "Haven't you noticed how strange he's acting today?"

I fire a look in her direction that could stop a grizzly in its tracks. She looks surprised. Hanging around Moss has made me stronger. As ancestors go, I've discovered I'm made from sturdy stock. But maybe not as sturdy as I hoped because Coltrane wrestles with my napkin under the table and wins. The meatball falls with a plop to the floor. Coltrane devours it before anyone notices.

We eat in silence, as I hatch my plan on how to get food to Moss without my mom catching on.

"Sorry about the concert, Quentin," *The Voice* says. "Maybe next time."

I'd forgotten about the concert. It has simplified things not to go, because of Moss. But I would never tell her that.

The phones rings and *The Voice* answers it. She's talking to someone and sounds serious. She looks in my direction. When she hangs up the phone, I can tell I'm in trouble.

"That was Mr. Richie," *The Voice* says to me. "He said you had a little trouble at school today."

A spaghetti noodle lodges in my throat. "What kind of trouble?" I cough to dislodge the noodle and push another meatball near the edge of my plate. Coltrane licks his lips.

"I think you know what kind of trouble, Quentin," *The Voice* says calmly.

Yelling I can take. But when *The Voice* gets soft it's scary. I stare at my plate.

"Who was this 'visitor' Mr. Richie spoke about?"

I freeze. Think fast. Think fast. Think fast, I say to myself, which stops any thoughts from coming, slow or fast. "He's a friend of Dex's," I say finally.

"Then why didn't Dex get in trouble?" *The Voice* asks.

My mom is smart, there's no question about it. *The Voice* starts asking questions and *The Look* joins in. My sister appears to be getting immense pleasure from Mom's interrogation. I don't blame her. I sound like an idiot. I let silence fill the space where my confession would go. My lips are pressed together so tight I have to remind myself to breathe.

"I'm too tired to deal with this tonight," *The Voice* says. "We'll talk about it tomorrow. But for now, no television for the rest of this month."

Since I was expecting jail time, this punishment seems like nothing. What she doesn't know is that I have the Discovery channel going 24/7 in my room. Considering how much worse this day could have been, I feel lucky.

"Can I have seconds?" I ask before getting up from the table. I make a point to sound contrite and hungry.

"It's more like thirds," Katie says.

"At least I don't pretend to eat like a bird then binge on potato chips in my room," I say to her.

She gasps, like she never knew I had this level of strength in me.

Mom refills my plate with pasta, a hefty amount of sauce and another meatball. Moss is going to love my mom's meat-balls.

"I'll eat this in my room," I say. Before *The Voice* has time to object I'm halfway up the stairs. I enter my room and latch the door, grateful to see Henry the VIII still swimming around in his bowl.

Moss sits on the floor and shovels in the pasta with his fingers. He crams the entire meatball into his mouth. Red sauce covers his face, mixing in with the grease from Dex's Honda. Even I'm disgusted. He lowers the last strings of spaghetti into his mouth, and then licks the plate. Coltrane whimpers, like Moss is trespassing on his territory.

"I guess manners haven't been invented yet, either," I say to Moss.

"I guess," he echoes, letting out a loud belch. "Burp, not throw up," he says. He smiles, then puts a sauce-covered hand under his armpit and starts pumping.

"No, Mom may hear us!" I say.

He stops. Pasta sauce hangs out in his ears and hair. I rummage through a pile of dirty laundry on the floor and find him a towel to wipe his face. He sniffs the towel deeply, like in the shower earlier that day, but then stops mid-sniff. This is not a clean towel. Not even close. He crinkles his nose and looks at me like he's not the only cave boy in the room.

"If you end up staying here, you have to learn how to eat without getting it all over you," I say.

"Stay here?" he asks. He doesn't look too happy about it.

"I don't know," I answer. "I'm going to try to dream you back tonight, but it may not work."

"Moss home," he insists.

"I'll try," I say. I feel responsible for getting him here but I still have no idea of how to get him back.

He drops his head to his chest. His grunt turns into a moan.

I dig my history book out of my book bag and show him photographs of cave paintings to cheer him up.

"Home," he says. He points to a cave picture.

"Yeah, home," I echo.

"Yeah," he says.

Mr. Richie's call and the attempted robbery are all I can think about. Moss, however, seems oblivious to all that's happened. I give him paper and a handful of big markers to draw pictures like the ones in the book.

I'm worried now that Mr. Richie will call Dad. But I don't even know if the school has Dad's number. A few minutes later, Moss shows me a picture he drew of his cave. "You're really good," I say. I nod and smile, pointing to the pad.

He's talented for somebody who's never picked up an art marker until today. I don't think I have any artistic talent, unless playing the saxophone counts. I smile as I remember Moss' amazing drum burst and our improvisation before our grand exit.

Moss hands me a marker and motions for me to try. I draw stick figures of my mom and sister. My mom's mouth is open really wide so *The Voice* can come out and my sister is bald. When I show them to Moss, he starts to honk again like the Canada geese have decided to stay. I have to cover his mouth so no one will hear and it leaves a spaghetti sauce imprint of Moss' nose and mouth on my hand. Moms and sisters must be the same no matter what time period you're living in.

"Are you all right in there?" *The Voice* asks from the outside of the door. "I thought I heard . . . honking."

Moss freezes. I reassure her that I am fine and make every effort to sound like my normal self.

"You've been in your room a long time," *The Voice* calls through the door. I see the doorknob turn, thankful I had the good sense to lock it.

"I'm cleaning my room," I say, thinking fast, but not fast enough.

"You are?" *The Voice* sounds happy and I realize the mistake I've made. Now I actually have to clean my room or she'll know I told a lie.

"I'll be out later, Mom," I say glumly. But the good news is her upset over Mr. Richie's call appears to have dissolved and she leaves.

I roll my eyes for Moss' benefit, which he imitates with perfection.

"Moms," I say.

"Moms," Moss repeats, rolling his eyes again.

If he ends up going home, I may be the inventor of the first pre teen rolling of the eyes.

I pick two handfuls of dirty clothes off the floor, wanting to kick myself for not coming up with something different to tell my mom. Even homework would have been better than this.

"Do you have to clean your cave?" I ask.

Moss snarls and grunts the affirmative.

"I'm glad I'm not the only one," I say. It helps to think of it as an ancient ritual performed by kids throughout the ages. I wonder what other ancient rituals we have in common. I bulldoze a pile of toys and books with my shoe, but there's still no sign of floor underneath. Moss' cave, from what I remember in the dream, didn't have any of this stuff. In a way I envy how simple his life must be.

"Can I come and visit you someday?" I ask.

"Visit someday," Moss says, then smiles.

"But I'm not wearing the furry underwear, okay?"

"Okay," he says. We shake hands.

"But I would like you to show me how to play the drums if you've got one."

"Drums," he says. He nods his head to agree, then smiles.

I wonder if Moss' head hurts from ramming it into that thief's stomach. He's been a hero today. I hope he rubs off on me before I try to make him disappear.

Cave Art

Later that night, I leave Moss drawing pictures and go to the bathroom to brush my teeth before bed. On the way back, the door is open to Katie's room. Her door is almost always locked, and I'm barred from entering for fear of death. One toenail inside unleashes her wrath: "Quentin, get out of here! Quentin, quit looking at me! Quentin this, Quentin that. . . ." She is *The Voice* in training. Despite all that's happened I feel drawn into her room, like one of those victims in scary movies, who go in the very room where the killer lurks.

"Come on in," she says, when I venture to the door.

What's going on? I wonder. Even Coltrane is allowed inside. He sniffs everything on his level. I plop down on a small square of uncluttered space on her bed between a stack of magazines and her pink book bag that looks like the explosion of a cotton-candy machine. The room is dark except for the eerie white glow of her make-up mirror and the small television flickering in the corner. The news is on. For a split second I'm surprised my sister is watching the news, but more than likely she was watching a program before it and just didn't change the channel.

Dex and I are convinced Katie is a vampire. Not only has she read *Twilight* a zillion times and has posters of all the stars of the movies on her walls, but she lives in a room barring sunlight and has two rather pointed bicuspids. But the mirror thing spoils our theory. Vampires can't see themselves, and Katie looks at her reflection at least a thousand times a day.

My sister being in a good mood makes the day seem even stranger. If I didn't feel so wide awake, I'd think I was dreaming again. As much as I hate to admit it, I like talking to her when she treats me like a human being instead of something to stomp under her shoe. An older sister comes in handy sometimes. For one thing, she's full of information on girls, because she's been one for years.

In an effort of good will, I resist calling her "Spazz," and thinking up new ways of getting revenge. For a split second I surprise myself and consider telling her about Moss and the robbery. But my temporary insanity abates. A total eclipse of the sun is beautiful but dangerous. A person can go blind.

"If I tell you something, will you not tell Mom about it?" I ask, risking the lesser of my two confessions.

"Sure," she answers, almost cheerfully.

I pull back the blinds to see if there's a full moon.

"There's a school dance coming up, and I'd like to ask someone," I say. It feels weird to confide in a person who tattles on me for sport.

"Quentin Moss," she croons, pleased with the secret she's been handed. Within seconds, I regret my decision. She looks in the mirror and basks in her conquest. Then she applies a splotch of white paste on her upper lip to bleach her unwanted facial hair. This doesn't seem fair since I've been waiting since

I was ten to get any small sign of a mustache, and my sister does everything she can to keep it invisible. Girls go to great extremes *not* to look primitive, I decide.

"How long have you known this girl?" Katie asks, now tweezing her eyebrows. I watch each pluck, amused by how barbaric it is to remove facial hair with tiny forceps.

"I met her today," I say. I'm fascinated with watching her wield the hand-held torture device.

"Today?" she asks, mid pluck. "You're moving a little fast, Q-Tip. You should become her friend first." She says this sounding as sophisticated as a person can when bleaching a mustache, tweezing eyebrows, and putting on a purple facial mask. "Get to know her as a person," she continues. "That's the only way these things really work out."

Okay, so this isn't what I wanted to hear. It sounds like the get-rich-*slow* plan to me when the get-rich-*quick* plan is what I have in mind.

"It works," she says with confidence.

I'm wondering if I can trust someone who cares more about her hairbrush than me. Meanwhile, my imagination presents me with another humiliating moment: I ask Alicia to the dance and she laughs in my face, making comments about Mr. Ed, as her new friends join in the laughter. My number one fear is history repeating itself. I imagine history repeating itself with Moss. What if I dream of Moss' cave again and instead of dreaming him back, I bring somebody else forward? My palms sweat at the thought of having two moms or two sisters in the house.

Katie takes off the mustache cream and proceeds to peel off the bright purple facial mask. This shocks me out of my current fear. If I had a camera I could put myself through college with the blackmail money.

"I've got to go," I say. All that purple stuff is making me sick.

"Suit yourself," she says, blowing a bright pink bubble with her gum. She glances over at the television. "Hey, that kid looks like you," she says. A special report is on and they're showing footage of the robbery. The convenience store must have had a security camera. They show Moss head-butting the robber in the stomach and are giving a number to call if anyone knows him.

I scream. Katie jumps.

"Why are you on TV?" Katie asks. "And who is that kid with you and Dex?"

I open my mouth to speak but nothing comes out.

"Mom's going to kill you," she says. Total satisfaction is written on her purple-tinged face.

"I've got to go," I say. I rush down the hallway, Coltrane nipping at my heels. I can't believe the one thing I was trying to hide—Moss—is splattered all over the television screen. Several thoughts rush at me at once, all involving the end of life as I know it.

Just when I don't think things could get any worse, I go back into my room where Moss has a surprise for me. I stagger at the sight and cover my eyes. I slowly open my fingers. Every single wall in my room is covered with life-size drawings of animals. "Oh. My God!" Katie is right. Mom *is* going to kill me. Or at the very least she's going to ship me away to relatives in the Hungary. I swallow another scream and close the door behind me.

"Moss, what have you done?" I yell in a half-whisper.

Moss drops the markers and jumps up on the window sill as if preparing to leap out to save himself.

"No, it's okay. Sorry, I didn't mean to scare you," I say. I pull him away from the window.

This latest surprise takes all the wind out of me. I slide down the wall at the feet of two six-feet-tall woolly mammoths whose tusks are locked in battle. I sit in the floor on a pile of dirty clothes and books and look up at the walls. It is a panoramic view of Moss' world and what a world it is. Strange creatures fly in the sky. Dark clouds are on the horizon, as the sun comes up over mountains. The drawings are large and vivid against the white walls. Life-size pictures of horses, reindeer and bison are in full gallop, chased by hunter's arrows. Moss is in the picture, too, standing next to a large cave overlooking a meadow and watching the herds. Next to Moss is me, complete with baseball cap and saxophone. At the bottom right corner is Moss' handprint, like he's signed the painting.

"Unbelievable," I say to Moss.

He looks at me like he wants me to say more.

"They're fantastic," I say.

He smiles, pleased with his first art review. Then he tilts his head like he's listening for a herd of giant elk. I can hear it, too. Footsteps up the stairs, two stairs at a time, as the most dangerous predator in the world approaches my bedroom cave. I break out in an immediate sweat.

"Lay down on the bed," I tell Moss. He does what I say. I throw a bunch of dirty clothes over him and rush for the door, but my mom beats me to it. She bursts into my room like a mountain lion cornering her prey.

"Quentin Timothy Moss," *The Voice* says.

I know I'm in deep dinosaur do-do if she uses my full name. But then her face goes white and she looks like she might faint when she sees the life-size drawings on the wall. Considering the tiniest crayon marks on my walls warranted no Sesame Street for a week when I was little, I can't imagine what this will cost me. I may not get to watch television again until my grandchildren are out of college—provided I live past this moment.

She stares at the life-size murals, her mouth open in a si-lent scream. I wait for her to ignite rocket boosters, hit the ceiling and go through the roof. Instead I am surrounded by an eerie silence that is much scarier than ten thousand rocket boosters. Under the dirty clothes, I hear the faint sound of Moss gagging, as if the smell has gotten to him. I start to hum *The Battle Hymn of the Republic* to cover up the sound.

"Quentin, what have you done?" *The Voice* says much softer than I expect.

"I can explain," I say.

She stares at Moss' drawings like someone drawn to the scene of a bad accident. I search my mind for an explanation that will keep me from becoming extinct. My heart is racing and my throat is very dry from all the humming.

"We're st-studying c-cave paintings in school," I stutter. "It's a school project. But I guess I got c- c- carried away." She knows I'm lying; I always stutter when I lie.

Moss moves under the clothes. I take a flying leap toward the bed, landing on top of him. He grunts when I land. I grunt, too, so Mom will think it was me. Then Coltrane starts sniffing where Moss is hiding. I push Cole away and toss a pair of dirty boxer shorts in his direction. He buries his head in the crotch with a satisfied sniff.

"Quentin, I'm worried about you," *The Voice* says. "I've never known you to be so, so primitive."

"I just got carried away, Mom. I'll paint over it, I promise."

The body squirms underneath me. I do a cover-up squirm. Pretty soon I'm gyrating like an army of red ants is under me.

The Voice tells me to stop and then gives me *The Look*.

I apologize and thump down hard on the bed to send the message to Moss that we're both in danger of rapid extinction. Meanwhile, my mom can't stop staring at the paintings. The last time I saw her stunned this bad was the day after Dad announced his plans to run away with the blueberry pancake lady.

The Voice asks what all my dirty clothes are doing on the bed. She walks over like she's going to fold it up and put it away.

"I was cold," I say. I pile the clothes higher without revealing Moss. Coltrane thinks I'm playing and begins to grab at clothes and growl. I throw a pillow at him and he stops.

"It's eighty degrees in here," my mom says. "Why in the world would you be cold? Are you sick?" She feels my forehead. "You don't feel hot."

I grunt and give her a shrug that Moss would be proud of. "I'll get started on my room right away," I say. I clear a path to the door like I'm rolling out the red carpet for her.

The Voice says we'll talk about this more tomorrow. I can tell she's still dazed by the pictures on the wall as she walks out.

As soon as Mom leaves I lock the door, and Moss throws off mounds of dirty clothes, taking in big gulps of fresh air.

"That was really close," I say.

"Close," Moss says.

In the next instant I remember the television report. "I've got to call Dex," I say.

Moss smiles. I think he likes Dex.

Since I'm not allowed to have a cell phone until next year, I grab the portable phone down the hall and bring it to my room. "Have you seen the news?" I ask Dex.

"No," he says. "Why?"

"It turns out the convenience store had a security camera. We're plastered all over the news!"

"You're kidding," Dex says.

"I wouldn't kid about something like this," I say.

"Okay, don't panic," Dex says. "Give me a minute to think."

I look over at Moss who is staring at the telephone like he's trying to figure out what it is. "It's Dex," I say to Moss.

Moss' eyes widen with horror, as though Dex has been shrunk to the size of a portable telephone.

"Calm down," I say to Moss. "He thinks you're actually in the telephone," I say to Dex.

"I don't know how you're going to explain this one," Dex laughs.

"Me, either," I laugh back. But the reality of the situation causes our laughter to fade. "Oh, and I've also got cave art all over my wall," I say, "except minus the cave. And Mom's already found it. She came in my room before I could stop her."

"I can't believe you're still alive to talk about it," he says. Dex has spent enough time around my mom to know her reaction to things.

"Barely," I say. "I have to clean up my room."

Dex, knowing the scope of this project, moans.

"But that's the least of it, Dex. Once she sees the evening news, I'll really be dead."

Moss circles me while holding one of my plastic baseball bats, like he's considering busting the phone open to get Dex free. I push him away, which is like trying to push a cement wall away. But he gets the message and stops.

"Oh, and you know what else?" I ask Dex. "Mr. Richie called during dinner."

"No!" Dex says. "Did he say anything about Moss?"

"He said something about my *visitor*."

"What did your mom say?"

"She asked who this *visitor* was and I said it was one of your friends."

"Oh great, now she'll come after me," Dex says.

"Not a chance," I say. "You're her favorite kid."

Moss is still circling, but at least he's put the bat down.

"Listen, I'll be over soon," Dex says. "But for now, unplug all the televisions if you have to."

"Okay," I say. Even though Dex is only three months older than me, he's the closest thing to a big brother I've ever had.

"And don't panic," Dex says. "We'll figure this out."

I hang up the phone and study the drawings on the wall. I haven't taken the time to notice how beautiful they are. These walls would be worth a fortune if anybody knew who really drew them. People visit caves in Europe and Asia all the time to see the same kind of art. I might be the only guy in the world to have genuine drawings by a cave boy on the wall of his room.

In the meantime, I don't want to think about what will happen if Moss is discovered. Among other things, my whole room might be dismantled and put into the Smithsonian. All of a sudden I'm wishing I could go back to a time before Dad left, when life was boring for days and months on end. I had no idea how great *boring* could be.

Paparazzi

"Don't panic," I say to myself for about the hundredth time. Moss looks with longing out the window at the azalea bushes, so I sneak him into the bathroom to avoid a repeat of this morning. I stand guard outside the door. After he finishes the longest pee in history, he flushes the toilet four times in a row until *The Voice* yells *Stop it!* And then threatens to come upstairs.

I stick my head inside the bathroom and he has a big grin on his face from watching the water swirl around inside the toilet bowl.

My sister comes out of her bedroom, and I freeze. I run down the hall and sequester her near the stairway.

"I need to talk to you," she says. "And you know what about."

"Later," I say.

"Not later, now," she says.

Moss sniffs from behind the bathroom door, and I am amazed at how far the sound carries. I throw in a few sniffs to throw Katie off scent, and she looks at me like I have brain damage.

"Why are you standing out here in the hallway?" she asks.

"Just headed downstairs," I say.

She gives me a long, skeptical look.

"I'll be in my room," she says. "Bring twenty dollars if you want me to keep quiet."

Sibling blackmail seems to be on the rise in our household.

I am about to go get Moss out of the bathroom when my mom comes around the corner. I almost jump out of my skin.

She puts a stack of clean laundry in my arms. *The Voice* tells me to put my laundry away and not to put them on my floor.

I hold my breath hoping Moss—who is at the other end of the hallway in our tiny house—doesn't grunt, laugh, or flush the toilet in the next few seconds. "Thanks, Mom, for the clean clothes," I say.

She feels my forehead again to see if I have a fever.

"I'm not sick, Mom. Can't a kid just be grateful?"

"Quentin, you're scaring me," *The Voice* says, dead serious.

"I'll put those away right now," I say, "and hey, let me take this stack of clean towels, too." I take the towels out of her arms.

She looks confused and walks away. I may have found a new secret revenge for when Mom's bugging me: niceness.

Finally, I walk down the hallway and open the bathroom door. "The coast is clear," I say to Moss. I find him standing in the shower, staring into the shower head waiting on the water to come on again. He's naked.

"Put your clothes back on!" I say. I drag him out of the tub and stand there until he dresses himself again. Then I pull Moss toward my room. We're a few steps away from safety when my sister bursts through her bedroom door and bumps right into Moss. We all jump, like a trio of Mexican jumping beans my dad bought for me once at a souvenir shop in the Grand Canyon.

I'm about to shove Moss into my room when she steps in front of him and blocks his path. My worst nightmare continues.

"Hey, you're the kid on the news!" Katie says to Moss. "Who are you?"

"Nobody," I say.

"Does Mom know he's here?" she asks me. "Does she know you're both on TV?"

"Of course she knows," I lie. "This is Moss. He's new at my school. I'm helping him get caught up with classes."

"His name is Moss? His first name is our last name? That's strange," she says, like she doesn't believe my story for one second.

Moss isn't saying a word, which is the smartest thing he could do. Meanwhile, Coltrane sniffs the crotch of Moss' pants for remnants of meatballs.

"I think I'd better talk to Mom," Katie says. "If she knows about this why isn't she screaming or something?"

"Wait!" I panic.

She folds her arms across her chest, eyeing Moss. "Who *is* this cretin?" she says.

Moss starts to growl.

"Is he growling at me?" Katie asks. She snarls her lip and shows her teeth.

Moss backs off. They're having a stare-off. A part of me wants them to go at each other just to see who would win.

"I'm telling Mom," she says again.

"No, no!" I plead. "She'll kill me."

Katie starts down the hall. I sink to my knees and beg her not to tell Mom. I cling to her skinny, Moss family legs and make no remarks about McNuggets or Colonel Sanders.

Instead of appearing pleased with her advantage, she looks worried. She glances at Moss again. "Q-ball, what kind of trouble are you in?" she asks me.

To my horror I start to cry. Quietly, of course, so our mom won't hear. Until now, I didn't realize how upset I was. In a surreal moment both Moss and my sister try to comfort me.

"Whatever it is, Quentin, we'll figure it out," my sister says. Her sincerity is about as shocking as having Moss materialize from a dream. "I won't tell Mom, okay? Now, tell me what's going on." We step into my room. I blow my nose on a dirty T-shirt and tell her everything.

I guess as far-fetched as it is, with Moss sitting there as proof, it's hard not to believe it.

"I think we should call Dad," Katie says. "He's good at stuff like this." As far as I know, our dad has no experience with time travel or cave boys, but I go along with it. Katie chews on her bottom lip. I wonder if she misses him as much as I do.

"Dad probably won't even answer the phone," I say, thinking that he's already deserted me right as I'm ready to hit adolescence, so why would he show up now?

"I'll try him on my cell." She narrows her eyes and gives Moss another long look before leaving the room. My panic seems more manageable now that I've confessed. While Katie is gone, Moss looks through another book at all the pictures. A few minutes later Katie comes back. "I left a message."

"What did you say?" I imagine a message that goes something like *Dad, Quentin's gotten himself in big trouble. He dreamed up a cave boy and now he can't get rid of him.*

"I just told him to call back," she says.

"Do you think he will?"

"He'd better. But in case he doesn't, let's think about what to do."

The three of us sit on my bed. We keep glancing at each other like we're waiting on somebody else to have a bright idea.

"The good news is," Katie begins, "that Mom is on a deadline and she's in her office working. She won't be watching anymore TV, and as long as he doesn't start swinging through the trees outside her office window I don't think she'll notice. Just keep your door closed."

"And locked," I add.

"Definitely," she says.

"Locked," Moss agrees. He leans over and sniffs Katie's hair.

"Oh, gross! What's he doing?"

"He's harmless," I say. "He just likes smells."

Moss moves in to get another whiff. "Down, cave boy," Katie says.

"Your hair probably just smells like something he would eat," I say.

"Actually, I do use a mango and papaya conditioner," she says.

"That's probably it," I say. I look over at Moss who is acting more interested in my sister with every second.

"We'll wait until Dad calls. For now, I'm going back to my room," Katie announces. She gives Moss a final look of curious disgust, and then studies his handiwork on the wall. "It's amazing the amount of trouble you've gotten into in just one day, Quentin."

"Tell me about it," I say. I walk her to my door. Moss joins us.

"So what is this going to cost me?" I ask Katie.

She opens the door and glances down the hallway to make sure Mom's not around. "For starters, you have to clean up my room."

I wince. Cleaning one disaster zone is enough, but two?

The Voice yells from downstairs, asking if everything is okay up there.

"We're fine, Mom," Katie calls back, cool as one of her cucumber facial masks.

The Voice makes us promise that we'll call her if we need her, and then she goes into her office.

"And since I just saved your butt again, you can wash my clothes, too," Katie says.

"Hey, that isn't fair," I say. She has the Mt. Everest of clothes piles in her room that way surpasses mine.

"Take it or leave it," she says, looking over at Moss.

Even though I feel like I've just been given two wedgies after gym class, I agree to do her clothes. It's humiliating to have to do whatever my sister says. I'm glad nobody's watching except Moss.

"Why aren't you saying anything?" she says to Moss.

Moss sniffs in her direction. Then he releases a cave-sized belch right in her face that reeks of garlic and spaghetti sauce.

"Neanderthal," Katie sneers.

"Exactly," I say back to her.

"By the way, I leave for drama practice at nine in the morning, so you can start cleaning up my room then."

Now it's my turn to look disgusted. "You say one word and the deal's off," I say to Katie.

"Your secret's safe with me," she says. "And tell your mossy friend he's got Mom's spaghetti sauce in his ears." She walks into her bedroom and closes the door. I usher Moss back into my room.

"Close," Moss says.

"Not close. We got nailed," I say. "But I think she'll keep her mouth shut."

"Nailed," Moss repeats with regret. He yawns.

While I wait for Dex I study the artwork on my walls. It's like a scene from an ancient movie. Bison are running and drawn in mid-stride. "Hey, you know these drawings are really good," I say to Moss.

Moss smiles. Then he yawns again, revealing all his bicuspids. I give him a pair of pajamas to change into that Mom got me for Christmas last year that I wouldn't dream of wearing. Except for his wild hair and bulging muscles, he'd look like a normal kid.

We clear space on the floor, and I put down a sleeping bag for Moss even though it's not even eight o'clock. The doorbell rings, followed by a loud knock. Coltrane starts barking like crazy. I tell Moss to wait in my bedroom and follow Katie downstairs to see who it is. Mom opens the door. A tall police officer stands in the doorway. For a second, Katie and I lock eyes.

"Sorry to disturb you, ma'am" the police officer says. "We had an attempted robbery in the neighborhood earlier today and from the video cameras inside the store we think your son and some of his friends were witnesses."

My mom turns to look at me, the shrillness of a three-alarm fire in her eyes.

I shrug to camouflage my panic. I begin to hiccup.

"It's one of his friends we're actually looking for," the police officer continues. "It seems one of the boys with your son stopped the robbery. It was quite impressive on the tape." The police officer smiles. "I'm surprised you haven't seen it on the news. The local station has been airing the video every hour, looking for the boy. The mayor wants to shake his hand."

I gasp between hiccups. Katie gives me a quick jab in the ribs with her elbow. Cars begin to pull up behind the parked police car. Reporters with camera crews get out and rush toward the house. I cross my legs to keep from peeing on myself. The cameras point in our direction.

The Voice asks what I know about all this.

I stutter something that sounds like I never learned the English language. I hiccup again. Dex fights his way through the crowd and slides past the police officer to enter the house. His eyes are open wider than usual and the effect of his eyes with his hair makes him look scared to death.

"Hey, you're one of the other boys," the police officer says. "But where's the third boy? He's the one everybody wants to talk to."

Dex and I look at each other. Katie and I exchange looks, too. The camera crews get closer. Now they're on the front walk leading up to the door. A couple of flashes from the cameras interrupt my panic.

"He's in the backyard," one of the paparazzi yells. The crowd, along with the police officer, followed by me, Katie, Mom and Dex, rush the backyard. Moss is in the tree house, leaning out one of the windows next to a big branch. The leaves soften his appearance, and since he's wearing those lame pajamas he could almost pass for an ordinary boy.

"There he is!" someone shouts. Camera flashes light up the nighttime sky like fireworks.

I stand frozen. Dex makes an audible gulp. Katie straightens her hair in case the cameras point toward her.

"Why don't you come down, son?" the police officer asks Moss.

Moss grunts. Murmurs go through the crowd. Moss looks down at me like he's asking what he should do. He's staring at the club in the police officer's belt. He stares up at the night sky like he's ready for this dream to be over. I walk over to the tree house and turn to face the crowd. All the cameras aim at me. Flashes come in blinding clumps. I smile--minus the gums--and raise myself up to my full height.

"This is Moss," I say to the crowd. "He's not from around here." I pause, unsure of what to say next. It becomes apparent that I need to buy time. "Moss will take all your questions tomorrow. He's had a big day." I sound like his publicity agent.

"Okay, let's break it up," the police officer says. He scatters the reporters, who take a few more parting shots. "I'll come by tomorrow morning at eleven o'clock," the police officer says to me. "Then we'll take Moss to meet the mayor. She wants to give him the key to the city. Moss is a hero, you know."

I yell for Moss to go back to my room. He climbs across tree limbs until he reaches the roof and then disappears through my window.

The police officer smiles and shakes his head like he's never seen anything like it.

It's almost midnight. Katie goes inside to get her beauty sleep and Dex goes back home, but not before promising to come over early the next morning so we can figure out what to do next. My mom makes herself a pot of coffee and sits me down in the living room. She makes me tell her the whole story.

There's No Place Like Home

To my amazement, my mom stays calm when I tell her about Moss. *The Voice* and *The Look* don't show up once. She asks how it happened, but I have no idea. I tell her that one minute I was dreaming and the next minute I have a cave boy in my room. I remind her about Grandma Betty's Hungarian gypsy theory and she rolls her eyes. She never really liked Dad's mom that much, but she agrees that sometimes life is a mystery.

I wipe my sweating palms on my jeans. Coltrane sits at my feet. He whimpers, like he's ready to go to bed and we're keeping him up late.

She asks about the robbery. I tell her about going to the convenience store for snacks. Any other time I would get in trouble for this because she wants me to come straight home after school, but she doesn't threaten to ground me for life or anything. I think it helps that my voice is shaking as I tell her. It's like she doesn't have the heart to come down on me too hard. And when I tell her about the attempted robbery, she gets a scared look on her face.

"It's okay, Mom. Moss was there. He wouldn't have let anything happen to Dex or me."

"They could have had guns, Quentin," she says. "I don't care how strong Moss is. If they had guns, you were in danger."

I think this must be a mom's worst fear: that their kid is in danger. For the first time, I think of how Moss' mom might feel having a kid of hers disappear into thin air. She must be worried sick. I stare at my shoes and wait for my mom to finish lecturing me on safety. I also yawn a few times and realize what a long day it's been. But despite the scary parts of my day, I don't think I would have changed a thing about it.

My mom sits thinking for a long time like she's trying to figure everything out. She assures me that we'll figure out what to do next as a family. I like thinking that we are a family again, even if we are short one crucial member.

"I need to see this boy," she says after awhile.

We walk up to my room where Moss has fallen asleep in the sleeping bag. He snores like his nose has the engines of a 747 inside. My mom's eyes widen and her mouth drops open as she stares at Moss. Then she slowly backs up so we won't wake him. She massages her temples like all this excitement has given her a throbbing headache. It's hard to argue with what happened when the proof is in my sleeping bag.

She reaches over to tame my hair. I let her. She says she's afraid of what might happen to Moss if the world finds out about him. This has been my fear all along, that Moss will become a modern-day circus freak and me along with him. I agree to meet with her in the morning to talk about how we can protect Moss. I like that she's treating Moss like one of her kids.

"Good night, Quentin," she says in the voice that used to read me bedtime stories.

"Good night, Mom," I say.

I get ready for bed. After looking at Moss' teeth all day, for the first time in my life I want to floss. But I dread what will happen tomorrow. Life has totally changed already. After tomorrow it could change even more. Moss will be exposed to the rest of the world. We could always say he left town. But how do we protect him in two weeks or a year from now? It doesn't seem fair to Moss. It's my fault that he's here.

I don't understand dreams. Who creates them? Where do they come from? If a dream can transport a cave boy to your room, can you dream them back? I look at the cave art again and notice a new figure standing outside the cave.

"Who's that?" I ask Moss.

He startles awake and his nasal 747s do a crash landing. "Huh?" Moss grunts.

I stand and point to the figure of a cave man.

Moss grunts and nods like he's glad I noticed. He pauses like he's searching his mind for a word. "Sha – man," he says.

"You have a shaman in your tribe?" I ask. I've read about shamans. There were the keepers of the magic in a tribe.

Moss grunts and nods.

"He looks a lot like you," I say.

"Fa – ther," he says.

"The shaman is also your dad?" I ask.

Moss grunts again in the affirmative.

"Cool," I say. I like knowing that Moss has a father, but even better than that, I like the idea that his father can do magic. We need all the magic right now we can get. Maybe his dad can help him get back. Since mine hasn't even bothered to return Katie's call, I doubt he'll be showing up to save the day.

"We need to go to sleep," I tell Moss. "I need to dream and we need your dad's help from the other side. Otherwise, you'll be meeting the mayor of Atlanta tomorrow."

"Mayor?" Moss asks.

"The mayor's nice and everything. But I don't know what will happen after that. Sooner or later someone will want to know where you came from."

"Not good," he says softly.

"No, not good," I agree.

Moss lies back on his sleeping bag.

"Don't worry about it," I say, trying to sound confident. "Now let's go to sleep. I've got some dreaming to do."

I turn out the light and about two minutes later the 747s in Moss' nose take off again. I can understand why he's exhausted. I'm tired, too, but the harder I try to sleep, the more I'm wide awake. I count sheep. I count Velociraptors. I count my teeth again and anything that might help me drift off to sleep. I ask whoever makes dreams to help. I ask Moss' dad, the shaman, to throw in a little magic.

I need my dad to say, "You can do this, Quentin." He always believed I could do anything I set my mind to. But I need to believe it, too.

Moonlight illuminates the drawings on the wall. I drift off into the dream world.

Moss stands outside his cave with his mom and a dirty cave sister with horrible hair. His dad, the shaman, looks up at the sky like he's thanking the sun god or something for getting his son home. His mom is so happy to see him she spits on her fingers and wipes the spaghetti sauce off his face. He looks irritated by the attention, but happy to be home.

I'm in the dream, too. I keep looking at my watch like I have somewhere to go. It's like I know I'm dreaming and I don't want to get trapped in Moss' life like he did in mine. I wouldn't last a day in this place.

"I have to go," I say to Moss in the dream. "Mom will wake me up soon."

Moss looks sad that I have to go.

"Quentin, friend," he says. Moss gives me his necklace made out of animal teeth as a sign of friendship. I'm trying to think of what I can give him, and hand him my Atlanta Braves baseball cap.

"I'll never forget you," I say to Moss.

"Never, you," he says back. He thumps his fist on his chest like we're blood brothers or something. I thump my fist on my chest, too.

Moss' dad makes me lie down on Moss' bearskin bed like we're running out of time. He gives me something bitter to drink and shakes my hand. My eyelids are so heavy I can't stay awake. I fall asleep. In my dream, Moss and his family wave at me from the front entrance of their cave. . . .

"Quentin, are you up yet?" *The Voice* yells up the stairs.

"I'm up, Mom," I yell back.

I sit up fast and wipe my eyes, looking around my bedroom. Moss is nowhere in sight. Where did he go? Did my dream work?

I cover every inch of my room to make sure Moss is gone. I lean over and look under my bed, but to get Moss under there would be impossible. I dig through a few piles of clothes on my floor and look in my closet. Boxes and clothes topple on me as I open the door. Then I look out the window to make sure Moss didn't just climb out into the backyard again. But Mom's azalea bushes are dry.

A familiar shuffle announces Dex in the doorway.

"I think it worked," I say to Dex. "Either I dreamed him back or his dad, the shaman, worked some magic."

"His dad's a shaman?" Dex asks. "How do you know?"

I show Dex the drawing of the man near the cave and tell him what I dreamed while I was there.

"Cool," Dex says. "Speaking of dads, your mom said your dad called this morning and he's flying home tomorrow for a visit."

"Dad's coming home?"

"According to your mom," Dex says.

I pause, remembering all that has happened in the last twenty-four hours and I'm grateful that Moss helped get my dad back, at least for a visit. "He was real, wasn't he, Dex?"

"As real as me standing here." Dex takes a closer look at the paintings on my wall.

"Hey, these drawings are awesome," Dex says.

If I need further proof that Moss was here all I have to do is look at my wall.

While Dex waits, I get dressed in my usual jeans and a T-shirt. I reach for my Atlanta Braves baseball cap, but it isn't on the bedpost where I always keep it. Then I remember giving it to Moss. I thump my chest in our brotherly greeting.

"You know, I feel a little sad about Moss being gone," I admit to Dex.

"Me, too," Dex says. "But knowing you, you'll dream up someone else."

"Don't even think it!" I say.

"Maybe you'll dream up some Italian kid named Leonardo who paints, too!" Dex cracks himself up.

"Not funny."

We stand looking at Moss' drawings on my wall like we're standing looking at a great work of art in a museum. I imagine

Moss in his cave wearing my baseball cap. He's working on a new cave drawing that has pictures of cars, zippers, and shower nozzles in it. When archeologists find his cave it's going to be the biggest mystery of the millennium.

"Hey, what's this?" Dex asks. He picks up a necklace of animal teeth next to my pillow.

"Moss gave it to me," I say to Dex.

"Awesome!" Dex says, as though envious.

We each try on the necklace and grunt and belch as we're wearing it. I look again at Moss' amazing artwork and for the first time in history I actually want to clean up my room to show off the drawings.

"Hey, you want to help me clean up my room?" I ask.

"In your dreams," Dex says.

Thank you for reading!

Dear Reader,

I hope you enjoyed *Quentin and the Cave Boy*. This is one of the first books I wrote after deciding to become a professional writer. It was written for children, however I have had many adult readers tell me they enjoyed it, too. The idea for the story came from a dream I had one night. In the dream the famous southern author, William Faulkner, came and sat at the end of my bed. The dream felt so real to me that I could feel the weight of his body on the mattress. The next morning, I wished he could have stayed with me to talk about writing. This idea intrigued me, and I began writing the story of Quentin who wakes up one morning with a cave boy in his bedroom. Also, as someone who loves to laugh, even at the silliest things, this was the first book I wrote where I gave myself permission to express my sense of humor.

I'd like to ask you for a favor. Please consider leaving a review of *Quentin and the Cave Boy* on Amazon, Goodreads, or Nook, iTunes, Kobo or elsewhere. Reviews help other readers take a chance on a book or an author they may not be familiar with. A review doesn't have to be long or "literary." Just two or three heartfelt sentences is enough.

You can write me at susan@susangabriel.com or message me on my Facebook author page: www.facebook.com/Susan-GabrielAuthor.

Thanks so much for reading *Quentin and the Cave Boy* and for spending time with me.

In gratitude,
Susan Gabriel

P.S. Do you want to get notified when I publish new books? I will email you as soon as I publish new books (two or three times a year at most). Please sign up here today: https://www.susangabriel.com/new-books/

Sneak Peek of
Susan Gabriel's novel
Circle of the Ancestors

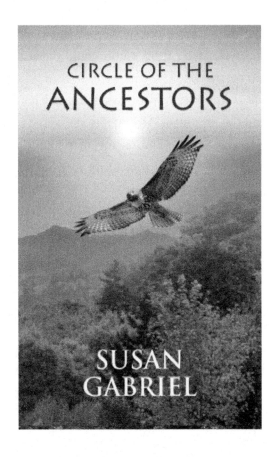

Chapter One

Morning light filters through the valley. Vast mountain ranges surround Sam like ancestors who circle to watch his every move. At times he isn't sure if they are here to help or hinder. He places a careful foot on the rocky path, letting each step settle before taking the next one, as his grandmother taught him. A misstep on his climb could mean a disastrous fall, or even death.

With slow and steady progress, Sam and his dog, Little Bear, ascend the mountain. Mountains are sacred to the Cherokee people and Sam's climb is meant to honor them. He reaches an out-cropping of rocks fifty feet before the grassy summit and stops to rest. Water from the last rain gathers in the cleft of a boulder and Little Bear drinks it. As a puppy he looked like a black bear cub, which is where he got his name.

"We're almost there," Sam tells Little Bear, but maybe he is reassuring himself. The climb is not easy.

As Sam pulls his way to the top, he thinks of how his grandmother would be proud. He wants to be a warrior someday. A real one. Not a fake one like his dad who poses in tribal costume in front of a souvenir shop near the casino whenever he needs gambling money. Tourists take photographs and leave tips, never knowing the truth.

Grandmother says becoming a true warrior will involve a test sent by the ancestors. Sam doesn't like tests, especially the ones he takes in school. But Grandmother reassures him this trial is different. It will call on all his strength and change him from the inside out. Sam likes this thought. He needs things to change.

At the summit—an altitude of 4500 feet—the vista stretches in every direction. Crisp air fills Sam's lungs and the early morning mist feels cool on his face. Fog nestles in the valley below, like a long, white snake zigzagging its body around the hills. Above the fog rises an orange and yellow sun cresting a distant peak.

"Hey look, we've got a visitor," Sam says to Little Bear, pointing to the sky. He blocks the sun with his hand to make out what looks like a red-tailed hawk. It is rare to see one.

For several seconds the raptor darts upward, as if racing with the sun to see which of them can go higher. The great bird holds steady against the wind, rising and falling on the currents. Its wide wings stretch like fingers reaching for greater heights. Rust-colored feathers ring its white chest. Sam stretches out his arms to imitate the hawk.

What's it like to soar? he wonders.

At the top he bows in the four directions as his grandmother taught him, thanking the mountain and his ancestors for letting him pass. He wonders why the mountain has called him here. It is simply to pay respect? Sitting on a rock, he eats the biscuit and honey he brought from home and feeds Little Bear the crumbs. Up here, life makes sense. People are small and unimportant and the landscape is what is great. The land doesn't have to pretend it is something it isn't to survive.

After completing his brief ceremony, Sam joins a narrow trail that descends the mountain in a different direction. He has never taken this path before, although his grandmother has told him about it. According to her, it was once used by Europeans who traded beads and blankets with the Cherokee. Through the openings in the trees, Sam sees the red hawk soar high above, as if intent on not losing him. The Cherokee are members of the bird clan, one of seven clans of the Eastern Band. Is the hawk a part of his clan, too?

A stream glimmers in the distance below like a tiny ribbon of light. Sam looks at his watch. For nearly an hour he has descended along the narrow trail that will end up a mile from his grandmother's house at a marked trailhead. Near a small waterfall the ground becomes slippery with moisture and moss. Cautious, Sam walks on the other side away from the ledge. He ambles through thick forest and the path darkens. Mountain laurel reaches up around him in all directions, a wall of deep green. The tightly closed buds are beginning to open and smell sweet and sour at the same time. It is easy to get lost in the maze of mountain laurels.

Two summers before, a four-year-old boy was lost in the forest. His parents camped on the north slope of Jacob's Ridge and the boy wandered off. The search continued for weeks. Forest rangers and volunteers, many of them from Sam's tribe, combed the entire mountain looking for him.

They found one sneaker about a mile from the camp and then all traces disappeared. The boy was never found.

Seconds later, Little Bear growls and then barks, his eyes trained on the trail behind them. Little Bear doesn't bark often, except to announce an intruder so Sam turns to look. A loud flutter of wings announces a swooping red hawk, its sharp talons extended. Wind from the bird's wings rush against Sam's cheeks. In the next instant, the hawk lets out a keening cry, like an ancient battle call. It swoops again. Before Sam can right himself he falls backward and loses his balance on the path. He stumbles toward the steep edge of the embankment. Meanwhile Little Bear barks wildly, grabbing Sam's pants with his teeth. For several long, slow seconds Sam clutches mid-air for something to hold onto, but he is too far off center.

Sam goes over the edge and lands with a loud thud on his back, the breath knocked out of him. His body quickly becomes a sled. He careens, feet first, down the mountain like an avalanche. The forest blurs past him. A voice—he can't decide if it is outside or inside him—tells him to dig in his heels. Sam obeys. He thrusts his hiking boots into the earth and slows his descent. A cloud of dirt and pebbles travels with him.

Trees blur past, then several large boulders. Sam hears a long, desperate scream and realizes it is his own. The stream, no longer in the distance, churns white water below him. Seconds before colliding with a large oak on the bank of the stream, Sam grabs onto the branch of a mountain laurel bush. He clings to safety and finally comes to a halt.

Waiting for the spinning to stop, Sam holds his head and sputters grit from his mouth. Little Bear barks from the trail high above him, sounding a continuous alarm. Sam is alive, but far from okay. His heart pounds like a drum delivering a warning. He can't remember a time when he felt more terrified.

Little Bear makes his way down the steep edge of the mountain creating cutbacks as he goes. For the first time Sam notices that he has fallen along the path of an old rockslide. Boulders lay nearby that would have killed him instantly if he had hit his head.

Small pebbles are embedded in his palms, as well as the moss and dirt grabbed on his descent. He brushes them away. Little Bear arrives panting and licks Sam's face. Blood trickles from a cut on Sam's cheek. He dabs the blood with his sleeve and grimaces. His head pounds as if running a race with his heart. He holds onto Little Bear like a life preserver. His watch is broken, stopped at 8:44 a.m.

On the ground next to him lies his red Atlanta Braves baseball cap. It was a gift from his mother before she left. He must have hung onto it as he fell. In a rare moment, he allows himself to wish she was here. He could use a mom right now. But life doesn't always give him what he needs. Sam brushes the dirt from his hair and puts on his cap, now dirty and torn.

His breathing returns to normal, although his hands haven't stopped shaking.

"I thought that was the end of me," Sam says to Little Bear. Somehow hearing his own voice makes him not feel so alone. Little Bear licks Sam's face again, as if he also thinks the fall could have been the end of Sam.

Like a puppeteer with a fragile puppet, Sam moves his arms and legs. Nothing appears broken, but everything hurts. That crazy hawk seemed to want to make him fall. He leans back to look for the bird, but it has disappeared. He will ask Grandmother if she's ever known a hawk to attack people. It followed him most of the morning, which is unusual in itself. To the Cherokee, birds are thought to be the messengers between the living and the dead. If this is true, what are the ancestors trying to teach him? How to die at a young age? Yet now that he thinks about it, didn't the last two days foretell that something big was about to happen?

About the Author

Susan Gabriel is an acclaimed writer who lives in the mountains of North Carolina. Her novel, *The Secret Sense of Wildflower*, earned a starred review ("for books of remarkable merit") from Kirkus Reviews: was also selected as one of their Best Books of 2012.

She is also the author *Temple Secrets*, *Lily's Song* and other novels. Discover more about Susan at susangabriel.com

Lightning Source UK Ltd.
Milton Keynes UK
UKOW05f2346230617
303989UK00001B/79/P